# What the press says about Harlequin Romances...

"...clean, wholesome fiction...always with an upbeat, happy ending."
— *San Francisco Chronicle*

"...a work of art."
— *The Globe & Mail*, Toronto

"Nothing quite like it has happened since *Gone With the Wind*..."
— *Los Angeles Times*

"...among the top ten..."
— *International Herald-Tribune*, Paris

"Women have come to trust these clean, easy-to-read love stories about contemporary people, set in exciting foreign places."
— *Best Sellers*, New York

OTHER
*Harlequin Romances*
by DORIS E. SMITH

# Wild Heart

by

## DORIS E. SMITH

*Harlequin Books*

TORONTO • LONDON • NEW YORK • AMSTERDAM • SYDNEY • WINNIPEG

Original hardcover edition published in 1976
by Mills & Boon Limited

ISBN 0-373-02071-6

Harlequin edition published May 1977

Printed in U.S.A.

# CHAPTER ONE

'Excuse me, but aren't you Victoria Elliott?' Victoria had noticed the inquirer at Vancouver being seen off by a nice family. 'Granny' going back to England after a holiday, she had thought. The guess was correct.

'My two granddaughters are fans of yours,' 'Granny' said.

'How nice of you to speak to me.' Victoria liked people. It was lovely to feel that many of them liked her. Not that she was often recognised like this. It seldom went further than a glance and the unvoiced question: 'Where have I seen that face before?'

Victoria's face—taffy-coloured quiff, cheeky nose and wide smile—topped most of her columns. She was a feature writer specialising in fashion. Though she mostly wrote about 'young' fashion, and looked the part in denims and a peaked cap, a recent highly praised series of articles had had a historical theme. Canadian television had interviewed her that week, so she supposed the image had been still fresh in her travelling companion's mind.

After they had chatted for a while 'Granny' settled for a nap and Victoria took writing pad and ballpoint out of her briefcase. The letter she was answering had chased her halfway round the world. It had set out from the Scottish Borders and it had come from her great-aunt Elizabeth Elliott. Though these days they saw very little of each other, the bond between them had been forged fourteen years ago.

That was the traumatic time when the car with Victoria's father and mother inside it had plunged over a quay wall, drowning both occupants. Lorraine, aged thirteen, and nine-year-old Victoria had subsequently found a home with their mother's married sister and her husband, but the surprise of that tragic summer had been an invitation for them from their father's aunt in the north.

'What do you think, Roger? Is it safe?' Aunt Helen had demurred. 'You know how odd Elizabeth is and the things she gets up to. Poor Mary always said she was extraordinary.'

Lorraine had shrunk from the prospect, but Victoria had been intrigued. 'Let her go if she wants to,' Uncle Roger had decreed. 'She'll get on all right. She always does.' So Victoria had gone north, and there could have been no better medicine for a broken heart.

Aunt Elizabeth had neither petted nor consoled; in effect, all she had said was: 'Welcome to my world.' And when it was a world of needy animals, there was no room for anything else. In the grey little town Elizabeth Elliott was a marked woman. At any hour unwanted cats or dogs would be dumped on her doorstep. Her bony figure in shabby blue tartan was a familiar sight round waste ground or derelict buildings. For four weeks Victoria's small one followed it on its works of mercy.

It was the start of a friendship that had defied the generation gap. They shared their pipe dreams; Victoria's was to go round the world, her great-aunt's was a cottage in Scotland. She loved the romantic Border country and had its lore at her fingertips. But since her fairy prince seemed 'to have missed the boat', it looked like being 'this poor old place for many a day'. As a child Victoria had, year after year, 'turned up like the summer' (it was her great-aunt's expression) at the 'poor old place' with its threadbare carpets, carrying-baskets and Cameron the marmalade cat, but latterly the annual visit had been impossible.

The penalty of having 'arrived' was that sometimes she did not see even her own flat in Bayswater for weeks on end. The tour just ending had been worldwide. A publishing group had commissioned her to cover the fashion scene in twenty different countries—enthralling, but gruelling on the tight schedule she had set herself. It was imperative to be home by the twentieth of July. That was tomorrow.

After that she was determined to take a break. 'So I could go and see her,' she thought. 'And I will.'

An added incentive was the address at the top of the letter. 'Wild Heart, Strathfin, Selkirk'.

On the last occasion they had met, two or three years ago, Aunt Elizabeth had been mysterious. Shortly afterwards, a change of address card had arrived with an invitation to come and take a look, but somehow work had always intervened. Aunt Elizabeth had understood; she had seemed almost as excited by the prospect of this last marathon as Victoria herself. Allowing for this, it was a little odd that she should have written as she had, yet the letter, in other ways, was so exactly Aunt Elizabeth that it furled up the years like a fan.

My dear Victoria,

Could you do with a kitten? I know you like marmalades. He is so pretty, most affectionate and will have a long coat. I found him on the doorstep, very thin and hungry. If you take him, you must promise not to let him out for a fortnight and after that never after dark.

There was a magazine at the doctor's last week with something by you in it. As you know, I have never gone in for fashion, but it seemed very good and I asked if I could have the photograph of you.

The kitten is a nice little chap and I will keep him

7

till I hear from you. Cameron died last winter. He was seventeen.

Affectionately,<br>
Aunt Elizabeth.

From a moment of bewilderment, ('But she knows the set-up. I wouldn't be there to look after it') Victoria had become convinced that the letter was in some way a cry for help, so inarticulate as to be a cover-up. Aunt Elizabeth had always paddled her own canoe, but she was not young and she could not keep up the pace for ever. 'She wants me to have that kitten,' Victoria thought. '*And* she's been to the doctor. Why?'

The reply had to be written with care. She instanced how long the letter had taken to find her and regretted that being 'a gypsy' put practical difficulties in the way of keeping a pet. Condolences on Cameron followed and some notes on the tour.

'I'd like to have had more time, but Lorraine is being married tomorrow, so I have to get home. Her fiancé's name is Michael Barnes, he farms near Carlisle. You can't imagine how pleased I am for Lorrie. She's a marvellous person, but I've been worried she'd never fly the coop. Anyway, once the wedding is over I'll be up to see you.'

Lorraine was waiting at Heathrow. Like Victoria she was fair, but there the resemblance ended. Victoria's licked-up quiff was golden, her eyes light brown, her face sunbronzed with Slav cheekbones. As a child, she had been 'the giddy one'. Lorraine was taller, a moonlight blonde, her hair shoulder-length, her eyes dark blue. Her label had been 'the good one'. She had run errands for all the elderly folk in the district and she had filled exercise books with stories which she would let nobody read.

Today a new glow in her face made her less ethereal.

'You look great,' Victoria said warmly. 'Where is he?'

Predictably, Lorraine had baulked at bringing the car in to Heathrow on her own. Michael was waiting for them by the exit doors, dark, tweedy, quiet and obviously very much in love. Victoria knew it was absurd, but she had had to see it for herself. Now she could give herself up to being happy for her sister.

Michael's mother was dead and his father was not coming to the wedding. He was in poor health and not up to the strain it would impose.

'Even if you'd had a quiet wedding in Carlisle?' Victoria asked sympathetically.

'We couldn't have disappointed Aunt Helen,' Lorraine explained. 'She's been marvellous. So have you, Vic. The dresses are super.'

As a change from writing about wedding garments, Victoria had sketched some of her own ideas and a friend in the trade had made them up. The genre was medieval. For the bridesmaids royal blue and gold brocade with bright blue Juliet caps and for Lorraine white chiffon with a square cut embroidered bodice.

She put it on and stood for inspection blushing like a child.

'Wonderful, isn't it—love's young dream?' Victoria teased.

'That's what it seems like—a dream. You do like him, don't you? Tell me the truth.'

'Do you mean to say you care what *I* think?' It was not the first time Victoria had felt the older of the two.

Disconcertingly, Lorraine did not laugh. '*You* wouldn't, I know, if you were in my shoes. That would be right somehow for you. But I'm older and I suppose not as brave. I want to be sure I'm doing the right thing.'

After months of hotels and apartments it was nice to be part of a family again. Victoria had accepted Aunt Helen's invitation to stay with them in Claygate until after the wedding. 'Longer if you like,' Aunt Helen had added. 'We'll be lonely, we're going to miss Lorraine so much.'

Victoria had always known that Lorraine, so like their mother, was her aunt's favourite and there was no doubt Aunt Helen and Uncle Roger had put their all into the wedding. The garden specially planted to give the lawn a wavy border of blue and pink. The marquee, striped in pale blue, with flower baskets hanging from the poles. The long trestles with flounces spotted in blue and blue candles in silver candelabra.

It was disquieting that the bridegroom seemed such a background figure—dazed-looking, even. It might have been an idea, Victoria suggested mildly, to have set the scene less elaborately out of regard for Michael and his anxiety for his father.

Lorraine looked worried. 'Do you think he minds? I couldn't say anything. It's their present to us.'

'To you, you mean,' Victoria thought affectionately. Lorraine had always been a perfectionist. It was plain she was revelling in it.

Victoria was just out of the shower when she was summoned to the telephone. The caller was Kevin Howard, an airline pilot whom she had met at a party in Singapore. She found him attractive but had not really expected a follow-up. The promptness was flattering. Kevin had leave coming up and asked if she was interested. They could go to Scotland if she liked, he would make himself scarce while she visited the old lady.

It struck Victoria that Aunt Elizabeth might like Kevin very much. She did so herself; getting involved was something else.

'May I ring you on Thursday?' she parried.

The thought crossed her mind at dinner that Michael might have had bad news of his father and was keeping it to himself. He kept studying his bride-to-be as though he was trying to spare her. Victoria supposed it was because she herself had always been, in the words of her family, 'nosy and pushy', but she knew that in Lorraine's shoes she would have had it out of him long ago. A trouble shared, after all, was a trouble snared. And yet she could have been wrong. Lorraine, who knew Mike better, was obviously leaving it up to him. Their love was not in doubt for a moment.

It was nearly bedtime when she remembered the letter she had written on the plane. 'Do you happen to have a stamp? I'd like to post this.'

'Yes, of course.' Aunt Helen went to her desk. 'But I'm afraid you've missed the last collection. Is it important?'

'I've a funny feeling it might be. It's to Aunt Elizabeth.' Victoria was about to elaborate when she noticed the startled faces. 'What's wrong?' she asked sharply.

'I forgot to tell you.' Lorraine had turned pink. 'She's dead.'

'There's nothing to mourn about,' Aunt Helen put in positively. 'Poor old thing. She had a miserable existence.'

That, somehow, was appalling. From a wool of pain Victoria had one crystal clear emotion. 'Miserable' was an insult. 'Existence' was another. Incidents she had not thought of for years came flooding back. The injured vulture Aunt Elizabeth had rescued in Egypt and kept for weeks in the bath. The brick that had been thrown through her window after she had given evidence in a prosecution for cruelty.

'Existence?' Never. You could say more truthfully: 'Forward the Light Brigade!'

'She was so brave,' Victoria said slowly. 'And so unselfish. If only I'd gone to see her!'

'Now that's silly. When did she ever want any of us?' Aunt Helen returned kindly. 'In any case, we're not going to discuss it now. Lorraine needs a good night's rest.'

Victoria had very nearly been in time. Aunt Elizabeth had died only three days ago from a heart attack. The funeral would by now have taken place. Lorraine gave the information when they were alone. She added that a solicitor had phoned but Aunt Helen had explained about the wedding.

'Did no one go to the funeral?'

'How could they? It was in Scotland. Besides, she was no relation.'

'I didn't mean Aunt Helen or Uncle Roger.' Victoria had always been aware that her mother's side of the family looked on Elizabeth Elliott as an oddity. 'I really meant you, Lorrie. Couldn't you have gone up? Couldn't Mike have taken you? I think one of us should have been there. We *are* the next of kin.'

'Do you? I never thought of that.' Lorraine looked conscience-stricken.

'It doesn't matter,' Victoria said wearily. She felt like hiding her head under the bedclothes and howling, but it was the last thing Aunt Elizabeth would have desired.

She had thought it would be impossible to put aside her heartache next morning, but she had not bargained for how full her hands would be. The five-year-old page in his white silk and blue velvet had somehow to be kept clean, the tiny flower girl showed unexpected temperament. The hairdresser came on time, but the bouquets were late.

The doorbell ringing brought general relief.

'It's all right. I'll go!' Victoria ran downstairs, her long brocade dress whisking from step to step.

She opened the door expecting to see freesias and white heather. The vicar, remembered from yesterday's rehearsal, was standing there.

'Oh, hello,' Victoria said brightly. 'I thought you were the flowers.'

Then she saw his face and it sent her heart into her mouth.

'I'm glad it's you, Victoria. I'm afraid I've brought you bad news.'

She remembered opening her lips and hearing no sound. Her knees felt cold and her ears hot as though they were going to burst. Then she was sitting on a chair and the vicar was talking. He was saying something about Michael having come to see him. He wanted them to know that the decision had not been taken lightly but with honesty and courage. There was a letter for Lorraine—he took it out of his pocket. They must decide who should give it to her.

Victoria sensed that he was kind and practical and would be a help with Aunt Helen. As for Lorraine, one would have to make oneself very calm ... and strong ... and wise—when in fact one was none of these things and would give anything to run away.

She stretched out her hand, took the letter and went slowly upstairs.

All this was in Victoria's mind a few days later as she headed north.

The news of her legacy from Aunt Elizabeth had been the third shock in two days. Apart from a small amount willed to an animal welfare society, it seemed she had inherited everything her great-aunt possessed.

The bequest had been couched in these terms: 'To my dear great-niece Victoria Mary Elliott, who through no fault of her own resembles me so closely, with love and most particularly without encumbrance.' In his accompanying letter the solicitor had stated that the phrasing was his client's own. If, as seemed probable, Victoria decided not to keep the property, he would arrange the sale. He hoped, however, that she would be able to come to Scotland soon.

Victoria had asked Lorraine to accompany her and, not unexpectedly, had received a refusal. It seemed cruel to persist, but she had done so. She was disturbed by her sister's attitude. Lorraine had displayed neither anguish nor a sense of injury. She seemed to be walking in a trance.

Michael's brief note had asked for two things, forgiveness and more time.

'Which means you've got to talk to him,' Victoria had argued.

'Talk to him!' Aunt Helen had echoed. 'Not if I've anything to do with it.' Lorraine, she added, must be taken away for a holiday. If Viccy wanted to join them she must promise not to mention Michael's name.

Kindness like Aunt Helen's could maim, and that was exactly what Victoria feared. In Scotland Lorraine would be a responsibility but that was beside the point. She had tried again.

'Don't ask me.' Lorraine had remained just as wearily adamant. 'You have loads of friends. Can't you get someone else?'

Kevin Howard, for instance, Victoria thought. As a matter of fact she was sorely tempted. 'I want *you*, Lorrie,' she said firmly. 'Please.'

That settled it, as she had known it would.

'How long will you be away?' Aunt Helen's mind had still been running on the holiday.

'As long as it takes to sell up.' Victoria could not be specific. It would be a sad task but inevitable. She hoped the local vet might advise on the animals, if indeed they were still there. Once they had been disposed of and she had gone through her aunt's belongings, the property could be auctioned.

She set off with Lorraine on Monday evening. It was easier to drive at night, stopping as required at transport cafés and snatching a catnap in lay-bys with the car doors securely locked. The morning rush hour round Carlisle slowed them a little, but they crossed the Border into Dumfriesshire very little later than planned.

'Welcome to Scotland,' Victoria said lightly.

It was a few seconds before Lorraine replied. 'I suppose it's time we changed over.'

They had arranged to share the driving, but somewhere between Liverpool and Kendal she had owned to a headache and Victoria had stayed at the wheel. Her heart had gone into her boots. Lorraine suffered from migraine and a bad go of it now would be disastrous. She had watched her sister anxiously as she swallowed the dope that was sometimes successful in warding off an attack and had then left her to doze. It was too dark to see the beauties of the Lake District and just as well for her to miss Carlisle with its unhappy associations.

'How does the head feel?' she now asked apprehensively.

'Not too bad.' Lorraine glanced at her watch. 'If I could just have five minutes in the air.'

'Sure.' Victoria slid the car into the verge. It was running very well; she had come back from abroad with thoughts of changing it, but there had not been time. The battery would soon need replacing, but it too was behaving itself. The car had been starting like a bird.

In short, the journey was almost over without incident. She hitched herself on to the wall beside Lorraine and looked about her.

The sticky night had given way to a brilliant morning. The hills were velvet printed, each gully distinct. Light sizzled on a field of yellow hawkbit. The Esk, its turbulence spent among the lonely Ettrick Hills where it had risen, flowed quietly over the stones on its way to the Solway. Canonbie lay behind them, Langholm and wild Eskdalemuir ahead.

Three horses galloping through a field were a throw-back to the stories Aunt Elizabeth had told. They had all been about this part of the world. Jock had won back to Hazeldean with his English 'ladie' and, a bit to the south, Allen-a-Dale had slept out under the stars.

Closest of all was Lochinvar, not only because he had been her favourite but because this was his patch. He had swum the Esk river and chased over Cannobie Lee. The years blew down like a stack of cards and she was nine again and soaking up the stagecraft—the goblet kissed, drained and dashed to the ground, the galliard so perfectly danced that it mesmerised friend and foe alike, and the final spring to the saddle. Somehow she had always pictured his horse as a grey.

A last nod to fancy. Did anyone care like that today? Kevin, she recalled, when he had phoned him to say that Lorraine would be going with her to Scotland, had drawled: 'That's it, then,' and rung off.

She blinked and called herself to order. Fifty miles had still to be covered, some on secondary roads, and with Strathfin not only off the main road but off the map as well, the navigator would need her wits about her.

'Would you like to drive for a bit and I'll watch the road?' She turned to her sister and for the second time felt her heart plummet. She had been foolishly optimistic. Lorrie was as white as a ghost. 'Did that stuff not help?'

'It may have done,' Lorraine said evasively. She had her hand over one eye.

'In other words it hasn't, so what's the next thing we do?'

'Forget I'm around, and that means taking my stint. Sorry.' Lorraine closed her eyes. She looked so wan that Victoria decided against rousing her in Langholm where they could doubtless have got a cup of tea. Her best bet now was to reach their destination and find her sister somewhere to lie down.

At first there were no problems. She took the B709 out of Langholm, followed the Esk upstream for some distance and then bore north to pass under the shadow of Jock's Shoulder and Wind Fell, and finally Ettrick Pen which topped them. The road crossed the moor and for miles her little car, which must have seemed like a beetle to the green hills looking down on it, was the only moving thing. It was desolate country, a memorial to the moss troopers and Covenanters who had ridden over it in years gone by, but it tugged at Victoria's heart.

The landscape mellowed as the road crossed the main one to Selkirk. There were heather slopes that would soon be a sea of purple, a scattering of farms and little houses which might have had something to do with the Forestry Commission, the River Ettrick and the Gordon Arms Hotel.

She went ahead, climbing with the twisty road. She knew the Borders only from their romantic past and the love Aunt Elizabeth had had for them, but it was extraordinary how they stirred and welcomed her. Perhaps that was her undoing. She felt so sure of her ground that she drove fast and confidently. Strathfin was off the beaten track somewhere in the Yarrow Valley between Traquair and Selkirk. She had been warned about its inaccessibility, but the feeling of adventure completely took her over.

It was a shock to find herself crossing the Tweed and

almost into Inverleithen. Strathfin, she knew, was not in this vicinity. What a fool! She must have come miles out of her way.

Reversing the car caused Lorraine to open her eyes. 'Sorry for doing a die on you. Are we there?'

Victoria had to confess that they were not.

'Oh well, not to worry,' Lorraine yawned. The pain in her head was easing, but she felt ''orrible'. 'The stuff I take gives you a sort of hangover. If I could just sleep it off I'd be fine.'

There was no chance of sound sleep with the motion of the car, especially on this hilly winding road, and neither did there seem to be anyone who might give directions. Victoria braked again. 'If I put the car into this lay-by will you get into the back and stretch out? I'm going into the bush!' Lorrie would have to lie down if it was only for half an hour. 'Not a brilliant start, I'm afraid,' she added humbly. 'You must be loving me.'

'It's okay, don't worry,' her sister returned stoutly.

Victoria spared a thought for Aunt Helen and how angry she would be if she could see them now. Lorrie had taken it very well, but with Lorrie self-effacement was the norm. Victoria was convinced that was at the root of the wedding débâcle.

First things first, however. She penetrated a farmyard and spotted an elderly man in an outbuilding milking a cow. It availed nothing; he was deaf and communication was hopeless.

The farm was on the edge of the moor and on the slopes behind it she could see sheep. There were stone pens on the side of the mountain and she remembered driving past a sign 'BEWARE YOUNG LAMBS'. It was faintly possible that the shepherd might be in the offing, though she knew that hardy hill flocks such as these needed very little attention.

And indeed the hope that had brought her out here seemed vain. On all sides the scene was the same, Blackface sheep, heather and shoulders of green hill. A lamb's bleat wafted on the thin air. Otherwise there was silence.

Suddenly it shattered. The bleating multiplied, becoming high and alarmed. Sheep that had been lying placidly scrambled up. And now she saw the reason. A large sandy dog had bounded in among them.

It was all play. The dog was a Labrador. Its long jaws were laughing and Victoria's immediate thought was: 'You big slob!' She whistled and slapped the leg of her jeans. No success. He was a fun dog enjoying himself hugely. The trouble was how to explain to the sheep. 'Bad dog!' Victoria said sternly. 'Come here.' He ignored her, but she wasn't too bothered. He was obviously a goodnatured dog.

And then the situation changed. She heard a thudding sound and glanced over her shoulder. A grey horse was galloping towards her across the heather. The man on its back was shouting: 'Call your dog, lassie! Call your dog!'

The next few minutes seemed to zigzag. Victoria yelled back: 'He's not mine!' The man came within seeing distance and reined up, his face changing. The dog backed, tail down, and snarled. 'Damnation,' the man muttered, and folded his lips.

They know each other, Victoria concluded brilliantly.

The tussle was short but memory-etching. The grey horse wheeling and turning. The flock driven across the moor. The dog separated from them and now disconcertingly at bay—an animal, Victoria deduced, as much anguished as angry. It seemed to be looking at its past. Aunt Elizabeth had had tales of dogs going berserk when life took from them the person who had

19

been their god. Or it could have been simply that the man at one time had illtreated it. Certainly there was memory of some kind.

She must have shuffled, because the dog rolled an eye at her and its jaws quivered apart.

'Just keep quite still, if you please, youngster,' the man bade. 'There is no danger unless you make it.'

Victoria opened her mouth and shut it without speaking. The horse's reins had been thrust into her hand with a brief: 'Thank you.' The man had swung himself to the ground.

The moment brought a clearcut and unpleasant discovery. She was afraid of horses. She had never been closely associated with them and they were very big. To keep her thoughts from the blowing noises which this one was making, she concentrated hard on the line of the man's broad shoulders. The belted corduroy jacket had deep pockets and as she watched he rummaged in one of them and pulled out a length of rope with a metal link collar attached.

'Sit,' he ordered.

The command, which obviously the dog knew, triggered off a further spasm—head down, teeth bared and suddenly a long howl more distressing to Victoria than anything which had gone before. It was the end of the struggle. The man repeated his order, this time placing a hand on the Labrador's hindquarters. In seconds the dog was sitting down and two brown hands were fastening the link collar round its neck.

Victoria was putting two and two together. 'Does he belong to you?'

'It's immaterial who he belongs to. He's signed his death warrant.'

'You don't mean . . .' It was a shattering thought. 'Oh, but surely . . . he hasn't harmed them. They're perfectly all right.'

'For this time.' Slightly amused eyes went from the pushed-back peak of her cap to her blue sneakers and trouser ends. 'By the intervention of providence—or its little finger!'

Victoria was in no mood for pleasantry. She respected the law that protected sheep, but good grief, look at the dog! She did so and it frowned. That somehow was the last straw. 'Could I not try to find his owner and explain?'

'Useless. I know this dog. He was ruined and now he's gone wild. Forgotten any training he once had and a danger to himself and the community. If I don't put him away someone else will.'

She supposed so, and that person might not be an expert. At least this way she sensed that the Labrador would not be at risk from clumsiness or cruelty. The trouble was his sloppy grinning face. 'I mustn't think about it,' she resolved desperately.

The man looked at her as he took back the reins she had been holding. 'Are you all right?' She nodded and he said surprisingly: 'Good girl. Now—who's with you? Shall I take you back to them?'

It took a second or two to find breath. She had a distracting vision of being mounted in front of him on the grey horse and returned in triumph to Lorraine, who would certainly think the migraine had given her hallucinations.

'*How old do you think I am?*'

'It hadn't occurred to me. A shock is a shock at any age. Are you alone?'

'No, with my sister. She's in the car.'

'Well then I take it you'll be all right.' He swung himself into the saddle. The Labrador whined softly, received the command: 'Come!' and got up.

'You said he wasn't trained. Look at him!' Victoria exploded.

The man glanced down unmoved. 'He's not to be trusted. I'll do what I have to do, lassie. Put it out of your mind.'

'Not as easily as you will,' Victoria thought sadly.

He looked like a man supremely self-sufficient. Strong features, boards of brown hair, a silent face. His eyes were deep set, their blue intensified by a leather brown tan. She pictured them looking along a gun barrel at a puzzled yellow Labrador and her heart turned over. There were scant grounds for hoping that this determined man would change his mind.

'I'll bid you good day, then.' He wheeled the horse round and the dog went meekly with the pull of the long rope.

'Oh, just a minute.' Victoria came out of her daze. 'Could you direct me to Strathfin? It's a village somewhere near here, at least I think so. It's not on the map, so obviously it hasn't got much to show for itself.'

'Quite,' he said smoothly.

The pause lasted only a few seconds, but it was enough to make her wonder what peccadillo she had committed and why he was staring at her so intently.

'You've come out of your way,' he went on. 'These days it's a closed road. Whoever directed you towards Traquair didn't know what they were talking about.'

'It was some years ago,' Victoria said evasively.

Sheer coincidence that the conversation should pinpoint the years she had let slip between Aunt Elizabeth's invitation and this sad belated arrival. Anyway, there was no use indulging in regrets, the important thing was to listen to the very clear directions she was now being given. Back to the Gordon Arms, turn left towards Selkirk, go as far as Broadmeadows and watch for Newark Castle. Soon after would come the narrow turn for Strathfin.

# CHAPTER TWO

As Victoria approached the car she was astounded to see her sister sitting up and combing her hair.

'Much better, thanks,' Lorraine said cheerfully. 'Did *you* have any luck? Let's get going, then. I've delayed things long enough.' She looked almost like her old self as she listened to Victoria's experience. 'I think you saw Lochinvar's ghost. Did he come out of the west?'

'North-east, I think. And no ghost, I can assure you. He means to put that dog down—rightly, I suppose, but I don't want to think of it.' Victoria hated to let it become an obsession, but she kept seeing the dog's face.

'There's no doubt Aunt Elizabeth will never die while you're around,' Lorraine commented. 'You won't get too involved, will you, Vic? I mean, you have your career to consider.'

Victoria was touched. 'No danger of that. I've too full a plate this autumn.' There were exciting things ahead, like the book she had been asked to write on period costume and the new series coming up for a women's magazine 'Shop with Victoria Elliott'.

It was eight miles from the Gordon Arms to Broadmeadows. The Yarrow Water threading the whins and the grass banks made a lace of blue, gold and green. The road curved gently under the rounded Lowland Hills. Away to the north-east an old drovers' track climbed its way to Traquair.

Newark Castle lay a mile further on. It could be seen, stark and roofless, on a green rise spiced with russet from the dying bracken. The horses and the hawks, the horns and the hounds had long since left it in peace, but its guide book description, 'a sentinel to the heart of the Scott country', still had power to thrill. Victoria would have liked to leave the road and go down to it, but Lorraine had just announced that she felt empty and suggested they should see if Strathfin had a pub where they could get something to eat.

The village was something of a surprise. The Douglas who had built it just over one hundred years ago (a group of cottages had the date 1865 carved above their porches) had had an eye for the picturesque. The inn yard sprouted hanging baskets of geraniums and the little garden round the War Memorial sparkled with pink petunias, bright blue lobelia and frilly African marigolds. A lantern hung from a post beside the kirk.

Victoria loved the unusual and there was some of it here—dovecotes made out of bleached wooden casks, a roofed circular seat round a sycamore, white candles in silver candlesticks on the stone walls of the kirk and little brass name plates on the panelled ones of the Grey Horse.

The licensee had known Aunt Elizabeth. He called his wife and they both reminisced about the wonderful work 'puir Miss Elliott' had done in so short a time.

'She really loved her animals. Such a shame the way things turned out,' Mrs Grant said vehemently.

Was it imagination that her husband cut in extra quickly with the directions Victoria had requested? Wild Heart was two miles away on the Devil's Elbow at the far end of the glen.

It was further from the village than they had expected and Lorraine suggested that it was stupid to pass the shop without buying what they would need. The shop shared the courtyard with the Grey Horse, and here again Aunt Elizabeth's name was the passport to instant friendship.

'She was a real guid soul,' the owner declared.

'There's no justice in the wor-rld,' one of the other

customers chimed in resentfully. 'Just think what some get away with!'

Background noises of: 'Ay, you're right there,' attended the ringing of the cash register.

Left to herself, Victoria would have found out then and there what lay behind the comments, but a warning nod from Lorraine checked her.

'Why did you stop me?' she demanded as they drove on. 'I wanted to know what they meant.'

'It wasn't the place for that. Anything you said would be round the village in no time, and you're not the silent type, are you?'

'Too right I'm not. And if I find out they've been slinging stones through the window—that happened before, you know, in the other house—I'll have them if it's the last thing I do!' She was suspicious, tired, angry and wanting to hit out. It made sense of a sort to put her foot down. The needle of the speedometer began to climb.

'It very well could be. Mine too. Take it easy.' Lorraine had been watching. She started in surprise as the car stopped. 'Oh! I didn't mean that exactly.'

'Neither did I.' Victoria had also been surprised—unpleasantly so. She pressed the self-starter and waited. Nothing happened and she repeated the process. 'Curse it, Lorrie, it's dead.'

The inquest was inconclusive. She lifted the bonnet and stared. It would not be the first time she'd improvised with a fan belt. Everything, however, looked right, tight and shipshape. 'I'll have to go back to the village.' She had seen no garage, but at least she could phone one from the pub.

'Let *me* go,' Lorraine urged. 'I've been resting. You must be exhausted.'

'No. It's too far for you. It might bring on another headache.' Victoria looked at the road devoid of shade and in blazing sunshine. How often in the past had Lorraine demonstrated that the spirit was willing but the flesh only too weak?

'I wish I could have had Kevin,' she thought, and hated herself.

At that instant, however, providence sent a substitute. A real live estate car was coming towards them.

'Those people in Mafeking,' Victoria said casually. 'I think I know how they felt.'

The rescue vehicle had only one occupant, a young man. His blond hair was smooth and brushed off his forehead, his face was long and clever. She liked him on sight, but at that moment even the Hunchback of Notre Dame would have looked attractive.

'Sorry for stopping you,' she said breathlessly.

The young man looked from her to Lorraine in a meaningful way. 'Don't apologise. When Venus is rising it always brings me luck.' He slid himself out of his own car and approached the casualty. 'What happened?'

'It was sudden death,' Victoria said sadly. 'And the P.M. revealed nothing.'

His eyes glinted appreciatively. Sometimes you met a person like that, on the same wavelength from the word go.

'Do you mind if I try her?' In the car he had looked tall, out of it he was exceptionally so. And not noticeably Scottish, she had to strain her ears to catch any intonation.

'It was quite funny,' Lorraine volunteered. 'I'd just told her to not to go so fast and I thought she was slowing down intentionally.'

'You're the keeper of the conscience?' He had a pleasant laugh and a warm way of looking at one. Unfortunately his efforts were no more successful than Victoria's own. 'I hate to say it, but I don't know. The only thing I can suggest is to take one of you to a telephone. Who'll be the lucky one? Conscience or keeper?'

Before they could reply the purr of another car sounded, this time from behind them. The road was not wide and Victoria stepped out of the way. A big car came round the bend, pulled out to pass and stopped a few yards away. The door swung open and the driver levered out. 'Can I be of assistance?' He walked towards them and Victoria's eyes popped incredulously.

A shirt, its sleeves neatly rolled, had replaced the corduroy coat and a faded kilt the breeches, but there was no mistaking the rugged face.

'What seems to be the trouble?' The cadence of the voice was as markedly Scottish as her memory of it on the moor.

'Sudden death I gather but ask her. She'll tell you.' The fair man handed over to Victoria with a smile.

'Yes, we've met,' the newcomer said drily. He walked over to the car. 'Have you run out of petrol?'

On top of frayed nerves it was too much. 'Look here,' Victoria exploded. 'How old do you think I am?' Cripes! It was exactly what she had said on the last occasion and, maddeningly, she could see he remembered.

'I don't know, but you seem remarkably anxious to expose my ignorance.' The blue eyes were now fixed on the dashboard. He tried the starter with ('Thank heaven,' Victoria breathed) the same lack of result. 'All right on petrol, if your gauge is working. When was she serviced?'

'Three days ago.' Victoria felt smug. 'In London.'

'Dugald will now tell you—never trust a foreigner,' the fair man put in.

Thank goodness someone was trying to lighten the gloom. 'Dugald'—it seemed a suitably unfrivolous name—was now peering into the engine.

'I suppose your battery isn't flat?'

'No, it's fine.'

'Hm.' He looked thoughtfully at the part in question. 'How old is it?'

'The battery is okay,' Victoria said distinctly. 'I know that.'

'You've had experience as a motor engineer?' The tone was conversational. He touched a wire.

'No, of course I haven't. I'm a fashion writer.' She felt angry at herself when she'd spoken. Angry and foolish.

'A fashion writer?' he echoed silkily. 'I see.' There was a little pause. 'How old is your battery? If you drive a lot in London you won't get more than two or three years.'

Victoria's battery was just starting its fifth year. She knew it was an astonishingly good performance and she was not a fool. She had mentioned it to the garage and they had said it was all right. She said so heatedly: 'In any case, a battery doesn't go flat suddenly, and I tell you I've had no trouble in starting.'

'That doesn't always follow,' the fair-haired man put in diffidently.

'I agree. Of course it doesn't.' Dugald pulled down the bonnet. 'I'll take you to Baldougrie. You can phone from there. There's an A.A. garage in the next village.'

'It would be quite sufficient if you would phone for me.' Victoria had no wish to spend a minute more than she could help in his company.

'It would be very foolish,' he inserted. 'You could have a long wait.'

She started to say that that would not matter and was as swiftly overruled.

'Fifteen minutes in this heat and it would matter quite a lot. Believe me, you'd grill. In any event what does your passenger say?' He looked past her to Lorraine, who as usual wanted to be placatory. She hesitated, her flushed cheeks contrasting with the lengths of straw-coloured hair.

'Oh, stop, suppose she gets a headache,' Victoria thought.

She had hoped for a counter offer from the first man, but disappointingly he now looked at his watch. 'Perhaps I should get under way, then. I have a call to make.'

'Yes, Craig, there's no call for both of us to delay,' Dugald declared tactlessly.

Victoria took note of the name. She liked it. It was a fad with her that names should fit the bearer. Her own had been a joke in the old days with her parents. 'How not to be a Victoria,' they used to say. Now she said warmly, turning to Craig:

'You've been so kind. Thank you very much.'

He looked amused. 'For nothing. However, I leave you in good hands.' Victoria's face must have shown her thoughts, for he added in an undertone: 'Take my tip, let him handle it. You'll get much better service.'

'Dugald' showed little reaction when she accepted his offer, but he handed them into the car and closed the doors with formal courtesy. Lorraine sat in the front, Victoria uneasily in the back. It was a foreign car, beautiful and fast.

'Craig Maxwell is our local vet,' Dugald observed.

It was news indeed. Victoria had hoped to enlist the vet's aid in disposing of those animals for whom she herself could not find homes. 'Living in Strathfin?' she asked hopefully.

'Beside the kirk. You may have seen it. The old manse, as a matter of fact. They didn't need all the ground, so they sold it.'

She recalled it, a charming house with white-framed windows and a spread of stabling.

The road had been steadily growing more wooded and twisty and they seemed to have run out of sign-posts. The car branched right at a fork and began climbing a steep gradient, narrow and unfenced with an air of privacy. From the left-hand window it was possible to look down on the road they had left.

'You would have carried straight on,' Dugald announced astonishingly. 'This is the way to Baldougrie. I'm Douglas.' It was said as though the name should be familiar. What made him think it was?

'Our name is Elliott,' Lorraine filled in with commendable poise. 'I'm Lorraine and she's Victoria.'

'The new owner of Wild Heart. Yes, I'd guessed as much,' Dugald Douglas said briefly. 'You're very like your aunt, Miss Elliott. I knew her very well.' Without turning his head he made it clear somehow that he was not addressing Lorraine.

The observation hung there stark as a withered branch.

The road ended at entrance gates, each pillar surmounted by a stone eagle. No name was in evidence, but as Dugald drove through Lorraine exclaimed in delight. Victoria, following her gaze, put a startled two and two together. 'Baldougrie' had sounded vaguely familiar. Now she knew why. It had been mentioned in the gazetteer to the road book, 'Baldougrie Castle, 14 miles from Selkirk, one of Scotland's inhabited castles'.

As castles go, the present building was young. Its turrets of red sandstone glittered against the bright sky. They had approached it from the rear, drawing up in a courtyard whose walls were swarmed by Virginia creeper. Five storeys of rosy tower crowned by a copper cone looked down on them from over the west wall.

'It's not always as quiet as this.' Dugald gestured at the neat yellow doors round three sides of the square. 'The dogs are mostly out exercising.'

The fourth side of the courtyard seemed to be an office. As they passed it, Victoria read the sign.

'Baldougrie Kennels. Breeding. Field and Obedience Training.
Proprietors: D. Douglas. M. McAlester.'

It answered a lot of questions. The man's nous, lack of fear and lack of sentiment. Dogs to him were primarily bread and butter. She wondered idly about 'M. McAlester'.

The office was empty and, mindful of Craig Maxwell's tip, she made no move when their host took up the phone and dialled a number from memory. Undoubtedly the garage got substantial custom from the castle. Dugald Douglas must be the laird of Strathfin.

The one-sided conversation was authoritative but courteous. Victoria gathered that the owner was not available and that orders were being left for him. 'Miss Elliott's niece. You remember Miss Elliott in Wild Heart? Yes, I thought you would.'

As Victoria started suspiciously, the unhurried tones went on: 'You could tell George, I think the battery may have died of old age. Miss Elliott has had it for over four years and she's just driven up from London.' There was a pause. Victoria could only guess at the comment from the other end, but it made Dugald Douglas's mouth lift at one corner. He raised his eyes unexpectedly and gazed blandly into her peppery brown ones. 'She tells me she's a—fashion writer,' he continued.

What made it intolerable was the smile Lorraine was trying to hide.

'Was that absolutely necessary?' Victoria demanded as the phone was laid down. 'You deliberately gave the impression that I'm a nitwit!'

'Well, candidly, in this instance, I think you are,' he

said with the same firm kindness that had mastered the Labrador. 'There must be an easier way of replacing a part. Did you not tell the people in London the journey you were setting out on?'

'I may have mentioned it.' To be truthful she could not remember. 'The point is, I'd have managed *on my own.*'

It produced a sigh of resignation. 'There speaks my old adversary Liz Elliott!'

It was no surprise. She had already sensed his dislike of Aunt Elizabeth. 'I'm sorry you didn't like my aunt, but I'm very proud to resemble her. She had to paddle her own canoe, but she always got there.'

'Indubitably, since she was no respecter of territorial waters.' Suddenly his tone changed. 'Well, that's the car taken care of. George Lennox is out on a job, his wife will tell him when he returns. Meantime, please make yourselves at home. If you'd rather look round outside suit yourselves. But watch for George Lennox, he'll come in here and I may not be around.' He left the door open as he went out. They saw him cross the courtyard and disappear from view.

Victoria sat on the table, lost in thought. She was very tired, (anger invariably had that effect) and disquieted. It had been evident from the remarks in the village that someone had crossed swords with Aunt Elizabeth. It seemed she had found the person. Such unequal sparring partners that it was a scandal. Dugald Douglas had so much. Aunt Elizabeth had always had so little.

The thought intensified when they went to view Baldougrie from the front. The style was Scottish Baronial with a soupçon of Restoration, most probably the work of Sir William Bruce. Clear light sharpened the stone garlands over the windows and the swaths and cameos that ringed the tower. Standing like a figure head on the prow of the glen, it sent Victoria's mind back to the times when a Borderer relied on the nearest great house for his protection and took the name of the family as a sign of allegiance. From such small beginnings Clan Douglas had become a power to be reckoned with in the Lowlands. If present events were anything to go on, things had not altered much.

In a surprisingly short time, George Lennox drove into the yard and, as Lorraine was being helped to climb into the high breakdown van, Dugald Douglas reappeared with two black Labradors at his heels and suggested that there was no need for her to join the expedition.

'You'd be wiser to stay here and let her pick you up when they're finished.'

'Oh, should I? I don't want to be a nuisance.' Lorraine's tone told Victoria that she would have liked to avail of the offer. It was a little damping.

'No fear of that,' Dugald Douglas declared. 'I'll be too busy to notice. But please yourself.'

'I think you should stay, Lorrie.' Victoria had got over the feeling of being odd man out. There was a drawn look about her sister's face that she had come to regard as ominous. 'What's the point in standing about? I'll come back for you.' She put her hand to the van, swung up beside George Lennox and slid the door across.

The garage owner had been watching the performance. Victoria's legs were not as long as Lorraine's, but they knew how to move. She couldn't remember when she had needed or been given a helping hand.

'Tell me something,' George Lennox invited as they got under way. 'Would you be a girl or a feller?'

It was his only lapse. He was a taciturn man and he worked over his patient in silence. Nothing could be done on the roadway. They proceeded back to the garage with the car on tow. Here, tests confirmed the trouble, there was not so much as a spark in the battery.

George Lennox broke his silence to ask in a wondering tone: 'How wis it you got as far as this?' When he followed this with: 'Whit was it Mr Douglas said you were?' Victoria had no doubt that in the minds of both men her classification was: 'Silly wee thing, head full of clothes nonsense.'

For all that, George Lennox had done his work and had wasted no time. They parted friends and he put her on the road for the castle.

Victoria did not put the car into the castle courtyard. She waited in the drive and clapped the horn. Dismayingly, it was Dugald who appeared.

'We were beginning to think you'd got George talking,' he said with a twinkle. 'It's a rare phenomenon, but your sister backed you to win.'

It was inconceivable that she was being paid a compliment, and yet she felt herself blush. He stood looking down at her and she felt conscious of how she must look, droopy shirt, hair sticky with heat, smuts on her nose. She had been trying to cool down by resting her arm on the window and now she saw the long smear of grease it had collected.

'Oh, it's so hot,' she said breathlessly. 'Thank you for letting Lorrie stay. I'm sure she would have been exhausted.'

'You're the one who should feel exhausted. Come and have a cup of tea.' To her amazement he opened the door of the car and gave her his hand. It was an old-world gesture in the style of the faded kilt. The question she had been expecting about the battery did not materialise, but probably his confidence in his own judgment needed no confirmation.

'A cup of tea would be nice,' Victoria said politely.

'But we mustn't delay. I've begun to despair of ever seeing Wild Heart.'

'I'll rectify that for you when we turn the next corner. You can look down on it.' He led her past the west tower of the castle and crossed a sloping lawn. It was well kept, ribboned by a recent mowing but innocent of flower beds. Dugald Douglas walked to the rim of it and paused. She saw that they were standing on the top of a brae which ended in woods many feet below.

'Do you see that white excrescence down there in the trees?' He pointed. 'That's Wild Heart. Your aunt was my nearest neighbour.'

Victoria's heart contracted as she stood looking down the tumble of pasture, brambles and bracken to the little house. In all the moments—and they had been many—that she had thought about Aunt Elizabeth since the news of her death, none had brought her so close. It was so perfect a setting for creatures needing sanctuary. How much it must have meant to them, and to the one who had come there from the grey streets of that dreary industrial town.

'I didn't expect this,' she said huskily. 'It's beautiful. Just the place for Aunt Elizabeth.'

Dugald Douglas was studying her, his head slightly to one side. 'Why do you say that?'

'Because dreams don't always come true so neatly. She wanted this for seventy odd years. The Borders were a sort of Utopia to her, and animals were what she would have given her life for.'

'Hm.' He had heavy lids to his eyes and they gave him a contemplative look.

If she was being doubted, it was intolerable. 'I've seen it.'

'I think you have rather a coloured view of your aunt.'

'Yes. All my views of people are coloured. By my own experience of them. I don't think that's particularly unnatural. In Aunt Elizabeth's case, love and kindness and an astute form of understanding just when I needed them most. Are you telling me, Mr Douglas, that you don't base your opinions on personal knowledge?'

'On the contrary, Miss Elliott. I'm telling you just the reverse.' It was quietly said and startling.

Victoria's brows knit. He couldn't possibly mean ... or could he ... As she opened her mouth he spoke again. 'And now that cup of tea. Come.'

The sinister undertones, real or imaginary, vanished as they headed back towards the castle. Three yellow Labradors came to meet them, two not yet full grown and weaving excitedly round their master. Very nimble dogs these, without an ounce of superfluous flesh and obviously laughing their heads off.

'Hey, beauties, you're making me dizzy!' Victoria protested.

'Youngsters,' her companion said briefly. 'With a lot of work to be done on them.' He snapped his fingers at the leaping pups and they subsided. The third dog kept at a distance. It had the look of a loner with thoughts of its own. It was very like the dog that had chased the sheep that morning, but Victoria was not sufficiently foolish to voice the thought.

'We thought we'd have tea outside,' Dugald Douglas vouchsafed at this point. 'This way.' If 'we' meant Lorraine and himself, it was a quick development.

The focal point of this second lawn was a summer house with a pointed roof and a weather vane in the shape of a Labrador. Inside the summer house Lorraine was ready to preside over the tea tray.

'So there you are!' Victoria said shortly. It was ridiculous, she knew, to feel taken aback.

Lorraine reported that Ellen Fenwick, who used to

give a hand at Wild Heart, was now working at the castle. She had seen her and Ellen had agreed to help them with the clearing out. 'She's coming to see us in the morning.'

It was certainly a welcome offer.

'You'll get your money's worth with Ellen,' Dugald Douglas pronounced. 'Deeds, not words, is her motto.'

'So I found out,' Lorraine agreed. 'But she spoke very highly of Aunt Elizabeth.'

'She would do. Your aunt was quite a charmer in her way.'

'That's the first nice thing you've said about her!' Victoria struck in.

'I repeat—in her way. She was a reiver and I had her at my gate.'

'Are you serious?' Victoria had never heard such nonsense.

Lorraine looked mystified. 'A reiver? What's that?'

'It's a cattle thief. He's mad,' Victoria pursued.

'Calm down. I used the term figuratively,' their host stated, unmoved. 'She was a Robin Hood, if you like it better. But this is no time for recrimination. She acted according to her lights. I always accepted that.'

'I think there's a great deal more you've got to tell us.' Victoria's head was swimming.

'Maybe. Now's not the time. She would wish, I think, to leave the glen in peace.'

Talk about the devil quoting scripture when it served him! Victoria opened her mouth and closed it again. It was one statement with which she could not argue.

But later, she told herself, later she would find out.

'Vic, do ask Mr Douglas to show you round Baldougrie.' Lorraine looked over as she put down the teapot. 'You'd enjoy it even more than I did.'

It transpired that, far from being too busy to notice

her, Dugald had taken her on a conducted tour. She had seen the dogs at each stage of training, some learning to retrieve, others working at scent discrimination and a sizeable number just there to be turned into what Dugald termed 'respectable members of society'. A separate area housed his stud dogs, all Champions, one of the bitches with a litter at the moment. The final division was the boarding kennels.

It was days since Lorraine had shown enthusiasm and Victoria was ashamed of her mixed feelings. This really did look to be good medicine.

'It all sounds very interesting,' she said carefully. 'But I'm afraid there just wouldn't be time.'

'Oh, not today!' Lorraine amended, laughing. 'I meant before we go home.'

'I've been talking to your sister about your plans for Wild Heart,' Dugald Douglas put in. 'I understand you'll be selling?'

'Yes. I don't seem to have much option.'

'None at all, I would think.' He passed a plate of scones. 'I'm afraid I underestimated your work. She has filled me in on that too. You obviously have a standing in your field. What I'm coming at is this. You want to sell, I want to buy. I hope we can come to an arrangement.'

'You want to buy Wild Heart? Why?' Victoria had no idea why it should have been such a shock.

'I could use the land and the cottage. Even though it may not look very convenient from this angle, I know exactly how I can fit it in. It's Baldougrie land, you see. Bluntly, I want it back.'

'You mean—Aunt Elizabeth bought it from you?' Victoria asked slowly.

'No. She had no dealings with me.' The tone had altered slightly. 'Four years ago my father was alive.'

# CHAPTER THREE

THE devil, who seemed in Victoria's travels to have more elbows than most, had yet another one at the exit to the glen. Wild Heart sat in its crook. It was bigger than either girl had expected and in excellent repair. Its brown-tiled roof looked almost new and the blue shutters were charming against the white walls.

'It's funny,' Victoria said, frowning. 'But I never thought of a modern house.'

'You'll get a very good price for it,' Lorraine remarked. 'It's really quite an inheritance.'

A natural remark but a douche of cold water, reminding that this was not a homecoming. The house had waited in vain.

'It's hard for you, I know,' Lorraine said gently. 'She meant so much more to you. I hardly remember her.'

'She must have wondered at times if *I* did.' Victoria let the door of the car slam. She was glad of the arm Lorraine threw round her shoulders as they walked up the path to the porch and the little light above it.

The house had been tidied. Victoria went through the downstairs rooms with a heart too full for speech. The cross-stitch cushion was an old friend. The cheeseboard hanging from a leather thong was a present she had brought from Greece. The picture postcards on the mantelpiece had all been sent by her—high cream and sienna gables from Amsterdam, an incredible peacock bay from the Ring of Kerry, white balconies from Barbados.

Soreness for any heart, but not the end. Upstairs the door of the back bedroom carried a small china plate. Its decoration—forget-me-nots garlanding an old-fashioned clock—was suitable for the period and the name it bore. It said: 'Victoria's room.' The promise was engaging, the room enchanting. It had broken away from the monastic white and had pale blue fitted cupboards and blossoms of blue and mauve in the wall covering.

'I suppose you realise this has been waiting four years,' Victoria said gruffly. 'I wonder what she'd say if she knew I was here now to sell it.'

'She *has* said it, loud and clear,' Lorraine reminded her. '"With love and most particularly without encumbrance."' She went to the window and raised the half-pulled blind. 'Here's something else she left you,' she said.

There was a strip of neglected garden with some crude hutches and pens and a gate leading into a field. The inspection parade was waiting—a small dog, hairy and reddish with very short legs, a tabby cat with very long white ones, four or five pullets and, looking over the gate, (Victoria's jaw dropped in amazement) a horse.

'What does one do with a horse?' she asked faintly.

Had there been the numbers she had been expecting, the task would have been greater but the impact less poignant. This little collection was pathetic. Ellen Fenwick had told Lorraine that 'the cruelty people' had taken away the rest.

'Apparently these belonged to Aunt Elizabeth. Ellen thought we might want them.'

Victoria could not work up much excitement about the hens. She felt guilty about not making a fuss of the horse, but she was afraid of it. The little hairy dog was no problem, it rolled a sad eye at her but was glad to come into the house. The cat growled and sat at a distance looking tall and sour.

'Those hutches and things are an eyesore,' Lorraine remarked.

No work or decision-making could be done that night, they were both much too tired. Lorraine laid the table while Victoria cooked supper. The aroma of bacon and eggs and sausages brought the cat to the windowsill, where it crouched, sniffing. Its nose was scratched. Someone, presumably Aunt Elizabeth, had taught the little brown dog to beg. It sat up first at Victoria's knee, then at Lorraine's, its liver brown eyes peering through a bunch of hair.

'Er—just in case you've forgotten ...' Victoria prompted, laughing.

Everything seemed better now that they had rested and eaten. It was sensible to remember the good times which had existed here rather than the present sad ones. Aunt Elizabeth had lived to see her dream come true and when her time came she had died among her friends.

Finding Wild Heart in such sound repair had lulled Victoria's fears. She would find good homes for the animals, but she would not allow herself to be torn apart. Wild Heart was a place of peace, it would be wrong to let it sadden her too much.

The little dog liked a fuss and didn't mind looking ridiculous. At the moment it was on its back in Lorraine's arms taking a rest after all the begging.

Victoria glanced over and was horrified to see her sister in tears. 'It's Mike, isn't it? Darling, why won't you talk to him?'

'Because it's over.' The old walled-up look had descended. 'I mean that, Vic, so don't try to bring us together.'

'Of course not, but I don't think it's in your best interests to stay permanently in Claygate. You need a place of your own and when all this is over I'm going to see you find one. Preferably somewhere where they'll let you have old Hairylegs!'

'Oh, I don't know.' Lorraine hadn't bargained for this. She looked despondently at the dog in her lap. 'I'm not sure I could manage him. Where would I go?'

'Anywhere you liked, but you don't have to decide now.' Victoria gave the drooping shoulders a hug.

'Sorry to be such a wet blanket,' Lorraine apologised.

'You're not.' Victoria was conscious that for the past twenty-four hours she had allowed her own problems to take precedence. 'Everything will be better in the morning. You'll see.'

She had every intention of following her sister upstairs within minutes, but at that point the little dog began to patter meaningfully from the back door to the front. A gruff little bark drew attention to the gravity of the situation.

Victoria smiled and opened the front door. Already the nights were drawing in and the flitting dusk deepened before her eyes. Hairylegs, a teacher's pet if ever she'd seen one, was quick over his business and soon ready to bed down, but she would have liked to see the baleful cat come in from the cold as well. A shadow in the bushes caught her eye and she followed it round to the back with the dog sniffing beside her.

Looking out towards the horse's field it was still fairly bright, but the crook of the Elbow was in woods and very dark. As Victoria walked down the garden she could have sworn that a figure moved round one of the hutches. At the same time a hen squawked indignantly.

Well, really! She might not have liked hens, but she was not going to stand by and see them filched from under her nose.

'I see you!' she called untruthfully. 'Leave those hens alone!'

The last thing she had expected was a reply. It came immediately in clear Scottish tones. 'That suits me fine, lass, but you'll not have one left if I do!'

Dugald Douglas came out of the shadows.

'What have I done now?' she asked resignedly.

'For pity's sake, girl, you've left your chickens out. How many do you think the foxes will leave you by morning?'

'My *chickens*?' For a second Victoria wondered. 'Oh, my *chickens*.' Those wretched hens were what he meant.

'Come on, let's get them under cover. How many should there be?'

She hadn't the least idea. He shook his head tolerantly and returned to the search.

'Did you come down specially to check on me?' Victoria asked, shooing one of the pullets from behind a bush. Not for diamonds would she have picked it up. Dugald Douglas handled them, she noticed, with speed and expertise.

'I came to check on the hens,' he corrected dourly. 'I taught your aunt how to mind them and I suspected history would repeat itself tonight.' He chased what appeared to be the last pullet into safety and shot home the rather gimcrack bolt.

'That was kind,' Victoria said breathlessly. 'Thank you.' She was touched in spite of herself.

'That's all right. The fault was Ellen's. She should not have left them out.' Ellen, it appeared, had been calling daily to leave food. It pricked home uncomfortably that the remaining inhabitants of Wild Heart had been depending on Baldougrie rations.

'I can see I have a lot to learn,' Victoria admitted. 'This is not my scene.'

'Carnaby Street would not be mine.' It seemed like an olive branch. It was also vaguely annoying. Not to disparage Carnaby Street, but she had written quite as many articles in academic vein.

'Will you come in? I'm afraid we haven't got much in the house, but if cocoa would be any good ...' It

43

sounded so ridiculous that she blushed. 'I was just going to take some up to Lorraine.'

He would laugh, of course, inwardly if not outwardly. He and his two resident assistants at the castle, both male as she already knew, would undoubtedly favour the national product for a nightcap. Strangely, he did not laugh. 'Cocoa would be fine,' he said gently. 'But some other time. You should be in your bed. You've come a long road today.'

It seemed a peculiarly peaceful moment.

'When we have more time will you tell me about Aunt Elizabeth?' Victoria asked suddenly. 'You said she was a reiver ...'

'At my gate,' he finished smoothly. 'See for yourself.'

A gesture sent Victoria's eyes up the side of the dark brae. Against the skyline lights were shining through the trees. She realised they came from the castle. An interesting discovery, but he had skated over her real question.

'Even if you didn't get on with her, I'd like to know about it.'

'We got on well enough,' he said shortly. 'My remarks this afternoon were ribald. I spoke in haste and I apologise. As a matter of fact I regretted her death very much.'

It was disarming. 'I've been trying to keep it in proportion,' Victoria hesitated. 'She was very elderly and I suspect not in good health. We all have to die. She did so peacefully in a lovely place.' Everything seemed to be straightening out in her mind. The remarks in the shop could mean nothing.

Dugald Douglas was studying her. Reading her thoughts, perhaps? Appraising that she would sell him Wild Heart? She had almost decided to do so.

'Yes. That too.' To imaginative ears it sounded a trifle forced. 'These things are not lovely.' He indicated the decrepit hutches. 'However, she did her best.'

Opinionwise, they seemed to be growing closer every minute.

'Are you sure you won't try that cup of cocoa?'

He smiled but shook his head. 'Not this time. I must be on my way. If you need further guidance you know where to find me.'

It was not so much offer as command. He threw her a wave and walked quickly down the road. There was a rough stone stile cut in the boundary wall and she watched as he mounted it. The bridle track it led to went on to the village. Dugald Douglas strode across the track and went with long steps up the side of the glen.

Next morning all was safe and sound, the horse standing quietly under a tree, the cat on top of one of the hutches and the chickens clucking in their house.

'You're not my scene,' Victoria told them as she unbolted the door and they picked their way outside. 'But I'm glad to find you looking so intact.'

Hairylegs didn't count because he had slept on the chair in Lorraine's room. Anyone coming to kill Hairylegs would have had to kill her first. No fool, that little dog, and very pleased with himself.

'There are flaws in your charter,' Victoria informed him sadly. 'But somehow I think we're stuck with you.'

Craig Maxwell would have to be consulted about the horse. The cat, too, though that seemed base. She rather admired the cat for not being in a hurry. It signified depth.

She had been first down, but only by minutes. Lorraine appeared in the kitchen as she was lighting the cooker.

'Scrambled eggs okay?' Victoria asked. Her eyes widened as Lorraine went straight to the back door, opened it and went outside. Victoria repeated the question, but it was a waste of breath. Lorrie was with the horse, fondling its head and letting it nuzzle her shoulder. 'Well, I'm blowed,' Victoria muttered.

'Sleep well?' she asked as they sat down to breakfast.

'Marvellously. There's a burn somewhere. I heard it,' Lorraine said cheerfully.

Victoria had prevailed upon her to buy the dark print shirt and the belted corduroy trousers she was wearing. It was not the dressy look Lorraine usually adopted, but it fairly thumped out its success. If I were writing about it, Victoria thought, I'd use the word 'liberated'. In simple terms, it was a great shape, long and lean, and she was actually envious.

'What about Dugald Douglas's offer?' Lorraine inquired.

'He hasn't made it yet. If it's fair, it's on.'

'It's bound to be fair. He's that kind of man.'

'You like him?' Victoria asked casually.

'Didn't you?' The ball bounced back equably. 'He was very kind.'

'I'm not sure.' She pondered the thought as she made her bed. Dugald Douglas made her feel a child. It was a foregone conclusion that he had treated Aunt Elizabeth in the same way, pointing out her errors and criticising the shelters she had contrived for the animals.

' "Sticks and stones may break my bones, names can never hurt me," ' Victoria reflected. It wasn't true— unless you had the hide of a rhinoceros.

She glanced absently towards the window and froze. The past was returning and while in that grey little English town it had been wonderful to be a part of it, she didn't want it now.

'Lorrie!' she called in consternation. 'Come here, quick. There's someone coming up the road with a basket!'

In the past four years many animals must have come to the doorstep that would never turn them away. This morning's caller—perhaps she had not yet heard of Aunt Elizabeth's death—was elderly, neat and sweet-faced with scraped back white hair. Lorraine took one look at her and laughed: 'It's all right. Relax. That's Ellen.'

'I am so very sorry that it is sad circumstances that have brought you to Strathfin.' Ellen Fenwick had the soft lilting voice of a Highlander. She stood in front of Victoria as though in recognition of her ownership of Wild Heart.

Victoria felt just as pint-sized as she looked. Five minutes ago bare brown feet and rolled up jeans with a carpenter's bib had not seemed out of place. Suddenly they did. The new arrival, however, had the kindest of light blue eyes.

'I would know you anywhere, Miss Elliott, from her description of you. She talked about you so often and she did feel proud.'

'But you were the one who was good to her, Miss Fenwick. Thank you for that.' Victoria glanced curiously at the basket.

'It is the kitten,' Ellen said simply. 'The one she was keeping for you. I was feared it would get lost, so I fetched it home.'

Victoria had assumed that the marmalade kitten had gone away with 'the cruelty people'. She felt slight panic as the basket was unfastened. Obviously so did the kitten, because it had crawled under the cushion Ellen had provided.

Placed on the floor, it sat like a butter ball until discovered by Hairylegs who gripped its woolly ruff and frog-marched it over the rug. From where Victoria was standing, you could see right down the kitten's throat. It took her two seconds to shout at Hairylegs and three to realise that his tiny captive was unperturbed. Obviously not just a pretty face.

It was not the moment to tell it, or Ellen, that it was not back to stay.

They had decided to offer Ellen any of Aunt Elizabeth's clothes that would be of use. Arranged for inspection, they spoke volumes about their late owner, only the bare necessities, clean but mended over and over again.

'Nothing has changed has it?' Looking at them, Victoria felt embarrassed and heartbroken. 'The last time I stayed with her I wanted to give her a present. I was in funds at the time and I thought a good warm coat would be the thing. But she never put it on while I was there, and the old one is still here. I'm sure she took it back to the shop and had the money for dog food.'

'She would do, Miss Elliott, she would do,' Ellen agreed. 'It was her way. And she would not wish you to grieve. It was better the way it happened than what might have been.'

There it was again, that hint, that whisper in the air. Victoria looked up inquiringly, but Ellen's face had regained its serenity. She had the stillness of her Highland race and still waters run deep.

Unlikely as it had seemed, she took some of the clothes, and when it came to going through the rest of the household effects she was a tower of strength. Victoria wanted to send as little as possible to the auction rooms and Ellen knew everyone in the glen and their needs. Victoria felt moved and inadequate beyond words. Here she was, knowing nothing and able to do nothing except dismantle.

'Please take a keepsake for yourself, Miss Fenwick. It's yours far more than mine. And try not to think too hardly of me for selling up. Mr Douglas has asked for the first refusal on Wild Heart. Did you know?'

'Oh ay. That would be natural,' Ellen responded tractably.

Victoria was glad that at that point Lorraine called up the stairs that she had made a pot of tea. The diversion gave her a chance to nerve herself. There were questions she must ask, and of all people in the glen Ellen Fenwick was the one to give the best answers.

She approached with care. 'Will you like working at the castle?'

Ellen had no doubts on that score. 'Oh ay, I have been very lucky. Mr Douglas has offered me a cottage, in good repair and nearer than my own. It would be a long way to walk in the winter from where I live now.'

'Don't answer if you'd rather not,' Victoria went on desperately. 'But I meant—do you like him?'

Ellen looked puzzled. 'Why should I not? He is Mr Douglas of Baldougrie, the family have been here in the glen for two hundred years. Dugald is the last of them now. There is no reason for me not to like him, Miss Elliott. He is a fine man and very hardworking. You will find no one in Strathfin to speak against Mr Douglas.'

'You mean, now that Aunt Elizabeth is dead?' Victoria asked gently. 'There was no peace between them, so I've heard.'

'It is true they had their differences, but I think the both of them respected each other. I have heard him speak about her as a bonny fighter and I do know she envied him his way with the dogs.'

'Was she ill? I had a letter from her when I was in Canada. It mentioned that she'd been to the doctor. I could go and see him, of course, but I thought I'd ask you first.'

'Dr Mackie.' Ellen was nodding. 'He told her to take things easily and not to worry. But of course she would not rest and she couldnae help but worry. All the kind deeds she did for folk, who would ever know they could land her behind bars!'

The spoon Lorraine had been holding tinkled into the saucer.

Victoria sat motionless, the words spinning in her brain.

'It was those old sheds she put up in the garden,' Ellen went on painfully. 'She had no permission, see you, from the council, and someone made a complaint. She had to go to court and they fined her five hundred pounds. She had a choice between paying it or going to prison. She could not pay, of course, and she would not take down her buildings, so it is my thinking that God knew best.'

It was a horrifying revelation, particularly to an imaginative mind. Victoria's showed her every facet, the shock, the grinding worry, the heartache, the fear.

Only one question remained—who had caused it?

Reluctantly Ellen allowed Victoria to drive her home. That she shared the anguish of mind over her late employer was undoubted, that wild horses would not stampede her private thoughts was equally so. Victoria knew she was up against the same silence with which four hundred years ago Highlanders had protected their prince. It made her think. Dugald Douglas was no 'Bonny Prince Charlie', but he was 'Mr Douglas of Baldougrie'. 'You will find no one in Strathfin to speak against Mr Douglas,' Ellen had said.

Pressed for her opinion on the identity of the person who had laid the complaint, she had been immovable.

'It would be just a guess I'd be making, and that would not be right. The good book tells us what harm the tongue can do.'

'Not everyone thought of that,' Victoria reminded her bitterly.

'No, but two wrongs have never made a right,' Ellen's voice, as always, was gentle. So was her look. 'She is at rest now, lassie. Leave it so.'

Common sense directed that the keepsakes should be deposited in Ellen's new cottage since she would be moving into it in a few days. When they left Wild Heart she directed Victoria to the right.

'Now right again,' she said after a few minutes. 'Past the big gates.'

Victoria glanced at the gates as she passed them. Their ironwork was exquisite, fretting into florets and true lovers' knots. An eagle clasped each pier and the iron frame was crowned by a coat of arms. The gates were closed.

'Where do they lead?' she asked.

'The castle. Those are the main gates of Baldougrie.'

'They're not open?'

'Oh no. You will never see them open,' Ellen answered unconcernedly. 'They have been closed for more than one hundred years. There are other gates at the back of the house for use.'

Victoria might have questioned why this should be, but at that moment her attention was distracted. A little girl was waving them down.

'Oh, it's Kirsty, Kirsty Connell,' Ellen said as they stopped.

The child was carrying with obvious effort a plastic shopping bag.

'That's a heavy load,' Victoria commented with a smile.

It was at Ellen, however, that the small girl was looking. 'Miss Fenwick, I've got it. Is Miss Elliott in?'

'What have you got, Kirsty?' Ellen asked with her usual unshattered calm.

'The black cat I was telling her about. The one she asked me to catch.'

'I see. Well, sit you down a minute and tell us about it.' Ellen had taken command and Victoria did not intervene.

It was the old familiar story. The cat had been spotted some weeks ago in poor condition. Aunt Elizabeth had asked Kirsty to bring it to her, but the Connell family had been away on holiday and it was only this morning that the stray had been rediscovered, ill and lying in a bed of nettles. In retrieving it, Kirsty had been badly stung, but all pain was lost in the joy of achievement. Victoria tried not to see the eagerness in her face as she inquired again about Aunt Elizabeth. It was like looking at herself fourteen years ago. The same thing had happened to her on rescue operations, but how little it had mattered.

Kirsty Connell must have been an ally, might even to some degree have taken the place she herself had vacated. Victoria could not watch the little freckled face as Ellen's news sank in. Suddenly she made up her mind.

'It's surely very simple,' she said loudly. 'I'm at Wild Heart. Give the cat to me.'

Ellen's new home was charmingly set with others in a gated yard which must once have been the castle mews. With Victoria's help she carried the various articles inside. It was near the time she commenced her daily work at Baldougrie, so she declined the offer of a lift back to the village.

'When I get the place to rights you must both come and have tea with me. That is if you will have time before you go back to London.'

'Heaven knows when that will be,' Victoria laughed. The flicker in Ellen's face confirmed a previous hunch. 'You're not pleased with me for taking that cat from

Kirsty,' she said boldly. 'I just felt it was the right thing to do.'

'Maybe. Kirsty's a fine wee girl and your aunt had a real soft spot for her. But if you will pardon the liberty, Miss Elliott, you'll need to be more practical. Don't take on too much, that's what *she* did, and look where it landed her. It's for your own good, lassie,' she urged as Victoria remained silent. 'Better folks should know now that Wild Heart is gone.'

The phrase echoed hollowly across the paved yard. 'I find the circumstances of its demise intolerable,' Victoria thrust. 'If I could trace the person responsible ...'

'They had the right on their side, mind. She broke the law.' Was it fancy that Ellen's gaze went a trifle fearfully over the terrace of freshly painted cottages? She would have much to lose if she were to speak out against a benefactor.

'Right, perhaps, but right out of all proportion,' Victoria accused. 'Miss Fenwick, I'm not wrong? You *were* on her side?'

It had not been a fair question. She regretted it when she saw the look in the older woman's eyes.

'Oh, lassie, if you had been here and seen her you wouldnae need to ask. But they are not bad men on the Council; when a wrong thing is done I suppose they have to act. And the truth is I don't know, not for sure, and so many have been good to me. So many are my friends.'

Victoria saw the dilemma. 'All right, I understand —and I'm sorry.'

She drove out of the mews slowly, finding her bearings as she went. The castle with its Gothic tower lay to the right, the kennels and the breeding block were behind it. Thankful that there was no sign of the king of that castle, she turned left. But fate was treacherous.

Dugald Douglas, a dog on each side of him, was striding across the grass. He waved an olive-shirted arm.

Victoria's return wave was sketchy. She had never felt less equal to the encounter before her, but she was on his land and it would have been awkward to pass him by. Besides, one of the dogs was frowning. She supposed that unless viewed through an owner's eye one yellow Labrador looked very much like another, but the thought was inescapable. That dog was almost impossibly similar to the one on whose behalf she had intervened yesterday on the moor.

'Were you looking for me?' Dugald called.

'No. Just leaving Miss Fenwick home.' Victoria broke off, staring. The dogs were near enough for her to see that each was carrying a thing like a little rolling pin with protruding nails. 'Won't they hurt themselves?' she asked a little censoriously.

'Assuredly if they hold too firmly, that's the general idea.' His eyes, several shades deeper than Ellen's, were quite serious. 'It's to correct what's known as hard mouth. A retriever who leaves teeth marks behind him is no use.' He said: 'Sit', and then 'Give'. The unfamiliar Lab obeyed promptly and received a word of praise. His companion sat, but made no move to surrender the trophy. Dugald Douglas said: 'Give' again and trod lightly on its toes. This brought the desired result.

'You don't approve?' he misinterpreted Victoria's intense scrutiny. 'Your aunt didn't.'

'My aunt?' She had sense enough to appreciate training and the rigours it imposed. She did not fancy the nail-quilted dummy, but certainly neither of these dogs seemed any the worse for it. 'Did she have words with you about it?'

'To begin with. Then she resorted to more efficacious methods.' He had been teasing the frowning dog with the dummy and now he tossed it across the grass. The dog went after his quarry like lightning. Once it was in his mouth, a long whistle blast summoned him in. He came and this time delivered when bidden.

The endearing brow lines put an end to all doubts. 'It is the same dog, isn't it?' Victoria challenged. 'The one you said you were going to put down?'

'And may yet have to. He's on probation. Yes, it's the same dog. Best I ever bred, but half ruined.'

'What a shame. Who by?' Victoria asked unwisely.

'The person who stole him. Your aunt.'

It was ludicrous. 'You don't really expect me to believe that?'

'Check with Ellen if you're interested,' he returned shortly. 'But don't let's labour the point. I was fortunate to find him again, he went missing two weeks ago and, as I don't need to tell you, could have been shot.'

'I don't understand. Do you mean my aunt had him at Wild Heart and after she died he ran away?'

'More or less, but I think she was beginning to realise that she had bitten off far more than she could chew. It's one thing to acquire a Houdini and quite another to retain him.'

'You paint an incredible picture of Aunt Elizabeth.'

'She was an opportunist, a reiver and a romantic. Most saints are. That's why they can never be canonised until people forget their nuisance value.' He looked keenly into her flushed face. 'It's an imperfect world, my lass. I have no doubt she'll be more appreciated where she's gone.'

'But sadly missed here, at least by some.' Victoria prepared to drive away.

He stopped her with the suggestion that they should go indoors. 'We have some things to discuss concerning Wild Heart.'

'I presume you mean the sale? Well, that I'm no longer sure about,' Victoria forced a calm tone. 'My aunt died of worry as much as heart failure. I learned that this morning. It changes my plans.'

'Meaning?'

'I may keep it on.'

'Then you would be crazy, girl! Though I can't think you mean it.'

She met this honestly. 'I want to mean it—if I have the courage.'

'Oh, lass,' he sighed. 'Do we have to go through all that . . .' His tone changed. He had noticed the shopping bag on the passenger seat and realised that a nose was poking through the zip fastening. 'What have you got there?'

When she explained, he asked peremptorily what was wrong with the cat. Victoria answered that she was looking to Craig Maxwell for that.

'You won't see him today. Wednesday is his day off.'

It was a setback, but it couldn't be helped. 'To-morrow, then.'

Reaction was unexpected. 'That could be too late. You have cats and you may be importing a killer disease. Let me see it.'

The examination, in a tiled outbuilding, was brief but carried conviction. Dugald Douglas handled the sick and sorry patient with an unsentimental gentleness. He had been looking for feline enteritis, he diagnosed something less lethal—cat 'flu. A well developed case with discharge from the nose and eyes and infectious.

'Almost certainly a high temperature. Needs a shot, but that must wait for Maxwell. Meantime these may help if you can get him to take them.'

Victoria looked doubtfully at the white capsules extracted from one of the wall cupboards.

'Quite safe,' he said, reading her thoughts. 'Simple

56

anti-biotics. We could take them ourselves. They won't be enough, mind, but they'll help. Get him to the surgery tomorrow and keep him isolated. That's if you must. You know my views on Wild Heart.'

'And I think you know mine.' Victoria took a capsule in one hand and tried to open the cat's mouth. It was a dismal failure. Ill as it was, the animal took hold on a new desperate strength.

She dreaded that her companion would see the effort it was for her, not only in skill but in overcoming revulsion. The cat in its present condition was not attractive. '*She* wouldn't have minded,' she thought with compunction.

'It's not easy,' Dugald Douglas said suddenly. 'None of it is easy, lass. That's the first thing to learn. And it takes two, that's the second.'

Devastating one minute, kind the next—that was the pattern he had already established in her mind. Now he took the capsule, opened the mouth gently by pressing the sides of the cheeks, dropped in the dose and tilted the poor head to assist swallowing.

'And another one,' he decreed, repeating the process. 'In case your delightful sister isn't up to assisting.'

By rights it should not have surprised her. She had sensed that the liking between himself and Lorraine was mutual, but the compliment was in such contrast to her own experience that she seemed for a moment to be looking at herself through his appraising eyes. The image was unflattering—a small grubby termagant in rolled up trousers.

'Your delightful sister,' he had said. It was a telling phrase.

# CHAPTER FOUR

CRAIG MAXWELL's premises were picturesque and had a pricey look. As Victoria had been told, they had once been the Manse. Now the minister lived in a small modern house and the long rooms and extensive yards of his former dwelling had been put to good use as a veterinary establishment. The surgery was open and she went in, basket in hand.

There were three or four patients and owners ahead of her, and once she mentioned her relationship to Aunt Elizabeth everyone looked interested. An old gentleman across the room vouchsafed that Miss Elliott had been the conscience of Strathfin, never afraid to speak up for those who could not help themselves.

'I suppose there's no chance you could keep the place going,' someone inquired. She looked inquisitively at the basket and Victoria, evading the question, explained what it contained.

She was soon made aware that she had come outside of clinic hours; Aunt Elizabeth, apparently, had had an arrangement, financed by an established society for Animal Welfare, for one hour a week of Craig Maxwell's time.

'If you go in now he'll charge you,' an elderly woman informed her. It sounded like a threat.

Victoria had just assured her that this could not be helped when the door opened.

Craig Maxwell had left a favourable first impression. This morning's was just as good—brushed-back fair hair, spotless white coat and a peacock of a tie. She caught his eye and smiled. It had an unlooked-for response. In seconds she found herself being ushered into the surgery out of turn.

'Miss Elliott has a special appointment,' he explained to the room's other occupants.

Victoria felt guilty. 'I didn't want you to do that. They were all there before me.'

'Nonsense. They've plenty of time. Most of them come for the crack.'

Craig Maxwell seemed in no hurry to examine his patient. He chatted pleasantly, inquiring if she was settling in at Wild Heart and suggesting that they might have a drink together some time soon. When Victoria confided her doubts about selling up immediately, he professed himself delighted.

'Tried to stampede you, did he? Dugald, I mean. He's like that. My best client, so I shouldn't say this, but at times a little overbearing.'

'I don't know what to do,' Victoria felt immeasurably relieved at having found a sympathetic ear. 'You see, I've only just discovered about my aunt's—worries.'

'And it has influenced you? Quite understandable. Well, I don't have to tell you, if you do decide to stay, anything I can do is yours for the asking.'

'That's a generous offer,' Victoria said gratefully. 'You may repent it.'

'Never,' he assured gallantly. 'What I don't do for you I'll do for your late aunt. I felt deeply sorry at the way things turned out. I'd like you to know that.'

'That's very nice of you, thanks so much.' It made a difference to find someone unequivocally on your side and prepared to show it. 'Now I mustn't take up any more of your time. If you could just look at this cat, I believe it has 'flu.'

The patient, if no better, was at least no worse, and for that she supposed she should thank Dugald's first aid. Craig injected it and expressed the opinion that it

59

would need further treatment. An appointment was arranged for Saturday afternoon.

On such a sociable plane money seemed out of place. Somewhat embarrassed, Victoria opened her purse. 'How much do I owe you for today?'

'Nothing,' Craig said easily. 'Wild Heart patients are on the house. Didn't you know that?'

'It was mentioned to me just now, but isn't there a special time for the clinic? I wouldn't want to impose.'

'I'll be the judge of that,' he smiled. 'But, for the record, in case you get inquiries, it's Tuesday evening, seven to eight. And you might put the word round that I'm a stickler for time. There's a general belief round here that there's enough and to spare of that commodity, but I wish I could find it!'

She could understand that, it was a common ailment among the medical and veterinary professions, and made her appreciate even more her own unhurried treatment.


The post had brought two letters, one for Lorraine from Aunt Helen and the other for Victoria from her agent.

'Aunt Helen wants to know when we'll be home,' Lorraine observed. 'She's still on about Italy.'

'Mirrie's on about Paris,' Victoria submitted wryly. 'I'm wanted for the collections next month.'

'You could fly from Glasgow.'

'You mean you think I could go?' Victoria could hardly believe her ears. 'You'd be willing to stay here and hold the fort?'

'Why not? It would only be for a short time and I'm sure Ellen would keep me company at night.'

'And Aunt Helen and Italy? I know she expects you home long before then.'

'Oh, Vic, don't pretend. It was all up with you wasn't

it the moment you saw this place. You've decided to stay.'

'Does that mean you'll stay with me?' Victoria had taught herself to be clearheaded. Lorraine had physical weaknesses and quite a different mentality. Could they do it? Was she tough enough? Was it fair?

She looked frowningly at her sister.

'Put it this way,' Lorraine submitted. 'It's not the Ritz, but it's not as bad as I thought.'

The words were almost drowned by a sudden knocking on the window, quite loud and most insistent. Lorraine, who did good housekeeping deeds instinctively, had drawn the curtains to protect the carpet from the sun. The sun itself helped to make the intruder's knocking less eerie. Nevertheless Lorraine paled a little. It was Victoria who put down her striped beaker of coffee and marched to the window.

The curtains went back with a rattle. They revealed the tabby cat looking taller and more tubelike than ever. Its narrowed eyes glinted above its white chest.

'Yes, puss,' Victoria said seriously. 'You heard right. We're staying. Welcome home.' She opened the window.

'Will you ever grow up?' Lorraine derided, shaking her head.

The cat taught them the ritual which obviously it liked to use. It pretended not to see the window and jumped down. When a puzzled Victoria opened the hall door it was there, but still not for coming in. As she watched it threw itself on its back and rolled voluptuously at her feet.

'It's got the sexes wrong,' Victoria called back. 'But it wants me to carry it over the threshold.'

Who was to know for sure what went on in the mind of an animal? But she had made the right guess. The cat clung to her purring quietly as she carried it into the house.

Difficulties might lie ahead, but the present was rosy.

Kirsty's black cat lapped some milk, they found three brown eggs in the hen house and talked to the milkman about supplies. Victoria made an appointment to see Aunt Elizabeth's solicitor, Lorraine went through the store cupboard.

After tea they took Hairylegs for a walk, kicked through a carpet of dry brown leaves, spotted the scarlet berries of woody nightshade and speculated on the different birds that whirred and piped in the undergrowth.

They had supper with the curtains open to catch the last of the day. The sky was a Spanish fandango as the sun left it and the wood looked as though it had gone on fire. The lights of Baldougrie twinkled in the gloom and in the armchair the kitten talked in its sleep and stretched out two barley-sugar paws.

Sentimental, no doubt, but to Victoria Wild Heart was already ceasing to ache.

The feeling of euphoria was still there in the morning. She made a start on clearing the papers in Aunt Elizabeth's desk, burning some and putting the rest aside for future perusal. Plans shaped themselves in her mind and a phone call to her agent in London was satisfactory. She would go to Paris as required.

In the afternoon, however, it became increasingly hot and stuffy. When they took Hairylegs out, he refused to walk, sitting down obstinately in the middle of the road. At home the kitten panted like a fox with its tongue hanging out. Victoria had never seen a cat pant before and it disturbed her. Loving them was easy, doing the right things for them did not, alas, follow automatically. Food was another problem. So far table scraps had sufficed, but a more balanced régime would have to be worked out.

Another bad moment came when Lorraine announced that she was going to lie down. It seemed that she had been fighting a headache all day.

Headache or heartache, Victoria wondered, as she put the tea-things to drain. It was useless to delude herself. The pain of losing Michael was far from cured.

The train of thought was interrupted by whining and a scraping at the door. When she went to investigate, the yellow Labrador, hero of Tuesday's chase, was outside.

Like owner, like dog. Ancient as Dugald's kilt was, he never looked scruffy in it. The Lab had the same quality. She read the name on his collar and smiled. It said merely: 'The Number Seven.'

It was not every day that seventy pounds of steel-bonded velvet came to call. Hairylegs was ecstatic. He stood on his hind legs patting at the Number Seven. He had forgotten that out on the road he had been too tired to budge.

The Number Seven bent to Hairylegs's dish and showed the white triangle under his tail.

Thoughts came instantly to mind. This was a play dog; would training ever eradicate what it most wanted to be, a friend of the family? Unquestionably this was why it had come to Wild Heart and why Aunt Elizabeth had kept it. Victoria's first doubts about her beloved great-aunt came at that point. Five years ago she would never have done such a thing. She would have seen it as enticement—or just plain stealing.

It added to her depression as she took up the telephone. A stroke of luck at last. Ellen was at the castle and answered the call. She seemed as anxious as Victoria to keep Dugald out of it and promised to ask one of the assistants to go down and pick up the escapee.

'It has happened before, hasn't it?' Victoria asked, tight-lipped.

'Yes.' Ellen sounded quite fearful. 'Yes, I'm afraid it

63

has. She was so very fond of the dog, you see, and she did not quite understand what Mr Douglas was doing with it.'

It was a chilling thought that her great-aunt, in her latter years, had so arrogantly taken the law into her own hands.

In one of the pathetic hutches she spotted the sign-board which Ellen had said they had taken down after Aunt Elizabeth's death. A demarcation line on the mast showed where it had been uprooted, but the legend was still bold and legible.

### WILD HEART ANIMAL REFUGE
### FOR ALL IN NEED.

Away—at least for the moment—went all criticism. It could not stand against the tide of love and sorrow. The board was battered, but it had still stood. Aunt Elizabeth had traced out that promise and had kept it —to the end.

'And I never came,' Victoria mourned. 'She might have listened to me, but I never came.'

The mute old board was suddenly a treasure. She shouldered it, found a spade and marched round to the gateway on the elbow.

It was not a professional job, but at least it was vertical and she had nailed her colours to the mast.

Flies were bothering Charlie, the old gelding, they had alighted on his forehead and seemed to be all over his eyes. It goaded her into putting a hand on his nose. The feel was quite pleasant, but unfortunately Charlie rolled back his upper lip and his teeth were long and terrifying.

Victoria snatched her hand away and stood rooted.

'Have you not got a piece for him? That's what he's looking for,' a voice called up the field.

Dugald Douglas must have intercepted Ellen's message and decided to be his own emissary. Vexatious enough without the added humiliation of knowing that he had seen her retreat from the horse.

She had no 'piece' with her, the cupboard she knew was singularly bare so far as equine tastes were concerned.

'Sugar would do,' Dugald suggested. 'I think I've some in my pouch.'

She was coward enough to hope that he had not, since instinct told her who was going to feel the touch of old Charlie's lips. Predictably she did not escape. Two lumps of sugar were retrieved from the round leather sporran and laid on the flat of her palm. 'Sorry I can't provide you with a bullet to bite on,' Dugald murmured. Unaccountably his look was gentle and so personal that she hardly noticed Charlie taking the sugar.

Many men had looked at her, none in quite this way. It was embarrassing that she could not control her rising colour, doubly so that he should notice it.

'I apologise for staring at you. You reminded me for the moment of someone I—once knew. It was not a question of physical resemblance, of course, just that she would never go too close to anything larger than herself.' He slapped old Charlie's quarters and sent him down the field.

A question followed on how they were progressing. Victoria answered confidently: 'Fine. I'm getting the hang of it now and we're clearing out the junk. Aunt Elizabeth, like most old ladies, kept everything. This, for instance. Don't you think the Wombles would love it?' The object in question had been cluttering up the hen-house; it was made of iron and cylindrical with a metal tube.

'Well now.' Dugald Douglas regarded it and her with interest. 'One good question deserves another. That is a water trough. When was the last time you filled it?'

It was wretchedly annoying and, worse, it could have been serious. Victoria was furious, with herself, with the water thing, with the silly chickens who could not use something nice and obvious.

'I hate hens!' she burst out childishly. 'They have it in for me!'

'Or *I* have? Is that not what you really mean?' Dugald Douglas asked quietly. 'Snap judgments may be an asset when you're looking at clothes, they'll serve you less well, I predict, when it comes to people.'

This could not go unchallenged. 'I'm not so bad on people, Mr Douglas, and it *is* my considered opinion that you look on me as a child.'

'If that offends you I apologise. Discourtesy was not intended, apprehension would be more to the point. However, you appear to have a great deal of resilience, quite enough by my reckoning to meet both waking and day.'

Victoria's silence was breathless and astonished. 'You're quoting Scott, aren't you? I can't quite think where.'

A gleam of approbation showed. 'Correct. It's the ending to his *Infant Chief*.'

She wondered would he continue and he did, his mouth quirking:

'"For strife comes with manhood, and waking with day."'

'I'm afraid my childhood was—interrupted.' Victoria had been oddly touched. 'And in my view long gone. However, I obviously missed out on one thing— water troughs!'

'Then I'll show you. It's automatic. Let me explain the principle.' He did so clearly and without rancour, also throwing in some hints on how the hens should be fed. 'Look after them and they'll repay you. They did quite well for your aunt. She made a profit.'

Victoria had been proud of the three eggs they had found; he chuckled and showed her how to look. One of the pullets invariably laid under the hedge. He went to the place and added four eggs to the ones he had already unearthed inside the hen-house. 'Even the hens have to prove him right,' Victoria thought sadly.

'Again I have to thank you.' She hoped the hurt of it did not show in her voice.

It might have done, for Dugald's strong features softened. 'There's no obligation lass. You're over the Border now. When we're neighbourly in Scotland we've generally a better reason than the thanks we may get for it.'

She felt small. 'I've really given you no reason to help me.'

'There's always bravery,' he answered drily. 'We have a national theme song about it.'

Mindful of past escapades, Victoria had confined the Labrador to the house. As she brought Dugald into the kitchen an ecstatic canine whirlwind all but knocked her flying. Dugald rapped out a sound of displeasure. Victoria could well understand that his strict discipline had not pleased Aunt Elizabeth.

'The Number Seven' was a quick-thinking dog. He bumbled round them giving the paw. He had done wrong, but he obviously found this a good way of fending off retribution. Somehow Victoria did not need to ask who had taught him the trick.

She thought even Dugald saw the funny side, for he smiled fleetingly as he secured his captive. If he left by the front road he could not miss the signboard. It would be easier all round if the resultant clash could be avoided. But to what point? Sooner or later he would have to know. And to go on benefiting from his guidance was sailing under false colours.

'Before you go, I've made my mind up. I won't be selling,' she said desperately.

Old Charlie had returned to the fence and Dugald had paused to rub his nose.

'Have you thought what's involved?' he asked.

'Yes. We've worked it out. Lorrie will do the house-keeping, I'll look after the animals.'

'You should weigh that carefully. It's a long way on, on your own.'

It was better than the reaction she had expected. 'You don't sound very surprised.'

'Not in the least. I told my partner we must be pre-pared to wait.'

It was the first mention of M. McAlester and, angry as she was at the implication that her surrender was only a matter of time, Victoria pricked with interest. Dugald satisfied it in a few words. 'Naturally he has to be consulted. He's in Edinburgh at the moment. I phoned last night.'

'There's no question of waiting, Mr Douglas,' Victoria said sharply. 'I'm sure your offer would have been a fair one, but I'm declining it.' No good would come of showing the antagonism she felt. 'And in the cir-cumstances I'd be more comfortable without your help. I expect you can understand why.'

'On the principle that gratitude erodes will power? I don't think you need worry.' He looked amused. 'But I take the point. However, I'm sure there's no need for us to be at loggerheads. I hope I may expect you at Baldougrie one of these days. I'd like to show you what I'm trying to do.'

The invitation was unexpected and disarming. Vic-toria was conscious of her pleasure. 'I'd enjoy that. Thank you.'

'Good.' He too looked pleased.

It was a strange moment. He had said it almost as

though he liked her and she had never considered such a possibility. Aunt Elizabeth apart, there was a special class of woman for a man like Dugald Douglas. A womanly woman, dancing the Gay Gordons in a long white dress with a tartan sash. Like Ellen of Netherby Hall who had danced the galliard with Lochinvar. She remembered suddenly those lines that epitomised romance and for some extraordinary reason it made her blush.

I look so awful, she thought.

Above them a window opened and Lorraine's head appeared. 'Hello! I *thought* I heard voices.' She came down smiling and looking a different person from the girl who had trailed upstairs only an hour ago. Trousers would never make Lorraine unfeminine, her heart-shaped face was much too pretty. 'Must you go?' she asked disappointedly as Dugald moved to the gate. 'Supper won't take a minute.'

'I'll remember that another time,' he said promptly. 'Tonight I've got work to do.'

It was good to see Lorrie looking happy. She fondled the Number Seven and told Dugald they would ring to arrange the supper date. 'You know we're staying? The die was cast yesterday.'

'I had heard.' For a second the blue eyes sought Victoria's face. Then they returned to Lorraine. 'I hope you'll be very happy in the glen,' their owner said courteously. 'Naturally we think the scenery in this region second to none. What about coming along the next time I'm going to a show? There's one coming up quite soon near Abbotsford.'

'Oh yes, please. How marvellous!' Lorraine's acceptance was ready.

'Well, that's fixed, then. Good. I'll give you a ring.' He opened the gate and steered the Labrador through it. Lorraine looked after them smiling.

*For quite a long time*, Victoria marked tolerantly. Was she hoping Dugald would turn his head and wave? Curiosity made her watch as the figures of man and dog went further and further away. Halfway up the brae they stopped. Dugald faced round and looked in the direction of Wild Heart.

He made a romantic silhouette as he stood, one foot planted on a boulder, his arm held high above his head.

There seemed no longer any mystery about her own invitation to visit Baldougrie. As Lorraine's sister he would certainly not want her in opposition.

# CHAPTER FIVE

STRATHFIN had had an anglicised air, Galashiels remembered its Border feuds. The town crest on the
municipal buildings showed two small foxes straining
to reach a plum tree and the hardly believable motto
'Sour Plums' was enscrolled beneath it. In 1337 a hand-
ful of English soldiers had been surprised while gather-
wild plums and killed.

Victoria had taken a devious route which skirted the
Gala Water. The country was green and undulating,
rich in rowan trees, oaks and sycamores. Galashiels,
like most towns in the Borders, had a flourishing tweed
and woollen industry. The mills in some cases stood
higher than the churches.

In the Town Centre the clock tower war memorial
was guarded by the statue of a moss trooper. Below the
clock was a figure holding a laurel wreath in each hand.
It is said that when daylight is breaking and when
darkness is falling the light throws a shadow from the
wreaths which makes the figure look like an angel in
flight. At the hour of eight the clock plays 'The Braw,
Braw Lads of Gala Water'.

Victoria had not expected applause for her decision
to re-start the refuge, but she appreciated that Mr
Lorimer had a professional duty to fulfil. He outlined
the rules which Aunt Elizabeth had broken like eggs.

'If only she had asked my advice this deplorable
business could so easily have been avoided,' he
lamented over a cup of coffee.

'If she had *taken* it!' Victoria put in mischievously.
'It *was* a deplorable business, as you say, but my aunt
was more sinned against than sinning. Witch hunt is

71

the word which occurs to me. And the word *I'd* like to hear is the name of the man who reported her.'

The solicitor looked reproachful. 'That is out of the question. Though most people, myself included, felt that it could have been better handled. Still, you disturb me, Miss Elliott. You've taken an emotional stand, I feel, with no account of the cost. I'm not un-informed about your sphere of work, my late client was very proud of you. It's far too much to give up.'

'I'm hoping it needn't be total relinquishment. More especially if I've inherited that fine. Have I?' It was an important question, one which she should have asked before.

'If you had I would have mentioned it at the outset.' Understandably, perhaps, Mr Lorimer showed a touch of asperity. 'The fine was paid anonymously before your aunt died. I hope I was able to set her mind at rest. I went to see her in hospital, but she was, alas, very ill.'

'Paid? By whom?' Victoria demanded.

'I said paid anonymously,' he reminded her gently.

It was another mystery. Who had dealt the blow? Who had sought to restore the damage? Victoria's light brown eyes made a vain search of the ones regarding her. The solicitor had been approached in confidence, he could not break faith.

A diversion was created by the arrival of Mrs Lorimer, who had come into town for Saturday shop-ping and was calling in hopes of a lift home. It involved a second round of coffee. Mrs Lorimer was an extrovert. She knew Victoria by repute and was excited at meeting her. She also knew Strathfin.

'That's where that poor girl was killed on the way to her wedding.'

'Oh no. How tragic!' Victoria exclaimed.

'Appalling. It was about six or seven years ago. She

was marrying Walter Douglas's son. I'm sure you've heard of Walter Douglas, he was a famous breeder and judge of retrievers.'

'Yes, of course I've heard of Mr Douglas,' Victoria said sharply. 'As a matter of fact my aunt bought Wild Heart from him.'

'Quite so,' Mr Lorimer inserted almost too promptly. Not that that registered over much in the shock of his wife's words.

'Well then, you'll know Dugald, the son. He's running Baldougrie now, but at that time it was much too tame for him.' The pause while she took a drink of coffee gave Victoria a moment to assimilate that six or seven years ago Dugald Douglas's bride had been killed on her way to marry him. It had a numbing effect.

But now Mrs Lorimer was off again, asking her husband to confirm that Dugald Douglas had been 'a James Bond'. The solicitor said resignedly that Dugald had been in Naval Intelligence. 'I don't doubt he had a testing and sometimes hazardous job, he would find glorification most distasteful.'

Yes, Victoria could imagine that. The fact remained Dugald had led an adventurous life.

'Oh well, the chapter's closed now,' Mrs Lorimer shrugged. 'He took over from his father three years ago. All he thinks about these days are dogs. It's a sad waste. Have you met him?'

'Once or twice.'

'Good-looking, isn't he? But he never married, mind that. She was his one true love.'

'My dear, your tongue is running away with you.' Mr Lorimer had been looking restive.

'No, John, it's quite true. Women understand these things better than men. He was the one for her and well she knew it, even if she did keep him hanging for years.

73

She would never have married anyone else, that's for sure.'

'I suppose she was very pretty,' Victoria ventured.

'Oh yes, she was *beautiful*. I never met her myself, but they said she was unforgettable. All I can say is, she was all that to Dugald. She refused him for years, but he never gave up.'

Victoria had a fertile brain. It worked tirelessly as she drove home. The wrecked bridal car was blurred, the other picture was agonisingly sharp. She saw it again and again. The kirk rustling with anticipation and up front the bridegroom waiting for his bride.

Behind it was another chilling reality. Dugald would have been trained to be hard and, where necessary, ruthless. More and more, in the case of Aunt Elizabeth, the finger pointed to him.

Forty-eight hours ago her sense of outrage had been unadulterated. Now it troubled her. There was a subtle difference.

Lorraine was another problem. Now that she knew Dugald's affections were so firmly entrenched in the past could she risk Lorrie becoming involved? A weight seemed to lie on her as she came to the glen. It was soon multiplied.

Two children had come to Wild Heart to leave their dog to be looked after while the family went on holiday. Lorraine had accepted the charge. 'I didn't know what else to do. They said Aunt Elizabeth minded it last year.'

'Oh, crumbs!' Victoria gazed in exasperation at the new inmate. 'I think that's pushing it a bit.'

'It was you put the board up!' Lorraine laughed.

It was clear that the table scraps from two people would not go round five resident animals and half a dozen pullets. Something else would have to be arranged.

'I'm bringing that cat to Craig Maxwell this afternoon. I'll ask him,' Victoria planned.

Craig, however, had a full surgery and no time to spare. Victoria held the patient steady and he injected it in the basket. She felt slightly let down that he did not compliment her on her nursing, but told herself not to be so silly. He was obviously 'up to his tonsils'.

All was very organised. You went in one door and out another. Craig held the exit one for her. 'Let's have that drink tonight. Are you free?'

It was a stroke of luck. 'Super. I want to pick your brains about dog food.'

'Dog food?' His smooth brow wrinkled in disdain. 'No way, my darling. We're not talking shop. Understood?'

She had more than a feeling that he meant it. It was flattering, but not what she most wanted. However, for the moment there was no alternative to some tins of patent food from the shop.

'Not very helpful,' Lorraine opined, when Victoria reported on the conversation. She talked realistically about the economies which would result from bulk buying. 'After all, we must be practical. At this rate we could have six or eight dogs before too long.'

Catering was a field in which Lorraine had always been interested. It underlined yet again the pity of having let Michael go out of her life. Aunt Helen was the kindest of persons, but her influence had been tragic. Lorrie had behaved and looked like a doll; she had never even believed in the woman she could be. Whereas now, after only six days in Strathfin, that woman was already peeping through.

It was disquieting to think she might be riding for another fall.

'You don't mind about tonight?' Victoria asked diffidently. She had felt awkward that Craig had not seen the evening as a threesome.

Lorraine's laughing assurance was, however, patently sincere. 'Enjoy yourself. Forget your troubles. You look great.'

Victoria was wearing a peasant dress which she had made herself. It was calf-length and full-skirted in a Liberty print that was mostly gold and orange. It had a matching shawl with a long sun yellow fringe. Victoria Elliott, fashion columnist, had suddenly come to the fore.

Craig was impressed. He told her smilingly that she would be wasted on the village pub and took her instead to a new roadhouse near Selkirk. It was a pleasant outing. He showed a flattering appreciation of her career and encouraged her to talk about it. Unlike all the others he saw no reason why she should be a flop in Wild Heart.

'On the contrary. Someone with your talents should find it a walkover.' His eyes shone wickedly and warmingly. It was the language she was used to. In fact, it was a great deal like having her friend Kevin Howard along after all.

'A toast to the memory of Aunt Elizabeth,' Craig said suddenly. 'For bringing you to Strathfin.' If, in the circumstances, it was flippant, she could not deny that it was also most agreeable.

'You said I mustn't talk shop, but there's so much I need to know. Dugald Douglas has been—kind, but I can't be under a compliment to him when I know he wants me to sell him Wild Heart.'

'I hope you'll never do that. Your aunt would turn in her grave.'

'What do you mean?' Victoria's heart thudded against her chest.

'Well, they were hardly the best of friends. He was

always sounding off at her for mismanagement. I'm certain she'd hate you to let him have Wild Heart, but I rely on you not to quote me. You may think that's cowardly, but the fact is I need his custom. So many people can't afford to pay fees these days, he can and does. Let's be fair.'

Victoria felt a rush of admiration. She had seen for herself how busy Craig was, but she had never dreamed that some did not pay for their animals' treatment. She mentioned half ruefully the dog Lorraine had accepted for boarding.

'*Boarding?*' Craig echoed. 'You mean *pro tem*? But that's not on, Victoria.' There was a slight change in his tone. 'There are adequate boarding kennels in the vicinity. You mustn't take bread out of their mouth.' He saw her flush and softened. 'Sorry. You'll think I'm getting at you. Please don't. You weren't to know.' He took a card from his wallet and handed it to her. It bore the name and address of a boarding kennels near Selkirk. 'Connections of mine,' Craig added. 'If it happens again I'd be glad if you'd recommend them. There's competition as it is with Baldougrie, Dugald Douglas takes boarders but has plenty going for him besides.'

It was another depressing instance of being out of her depth. A thousand pities that Aunt Elizabeth had left no guidelines.

'This is a case in point,' Victoria sighed. 'If only I could speak to someone who knew how she operated.'

'Jim Redfern!' Craig said abruptly. 'Works on the local rag and knew Wild Heart inside out. He used to give your aunt a write-up when she had animals that wanted homes. Yes.' He looked at her thoughtfully. 'Why didn't I think of that earlier? Jim Redfern. The very man.'

It seemed like an answer to prayer.

Craig declined an invitation to come in for coffee and

77

renew acquaintance with Lorraine. Victoria thanked him again and went up the path. Wild Heart was in darkness.

The hall light revealed only the kitten peeping round round a corner. Its cluck of joy when it saw her suggested that it had been left alone in the house. True enough, Lorraine was missing. The dogs were barking from one of the outhouses and the pullets had been shut up.

Victoria, puzzled but telling herself not to fuss, was just turning back into the house when she saw a horse coming out of the trees on the far side of the elbow. As it aproached, she distinguished the two figures on its back, Dugald Douglas holding the reins and in front of him Lorraine.

'Lorrie, is something wrong?' Victoria's first thought was that Dugald was bringing home a casualty. She hurried out of the gateway, her shawl's long fringe tossing silkily.

Lorraine was laughing: 'Of course not. Dugald gave me a lift, that's all.'

Victoria watched as Dugald first swung himself to the ground and then 'landed' his passenger. Had it been anyone but him, she would have rejoiced to see the sparkle in her sister's eyes. But suddenly she became aware of scrutiny. Dugald was looking her up and down.

'You have a second sister, Lorraine? One I've not met before.'

It took Victoria a second to 'catch on'.

'I just know the wee one,' Dugald continued. With perfect gravity he extended his hand. 'Delighted to meet you at last, Miss Elliott.'

It was a half truth. Victoria knew he would welcome a change in their relations. But that condescending 'wee one' was hard to stomach. For all that, short of

78

violence, she couldn't prevent him clasping her hand. It was another addition to that necklace of strange moments.

'You'll be glad to hear I've solved one of our problems.' Lorraine had gone round to fondle the horse's head. 'Dugald says we should buy the dogs' meat in bulk and store it in his freezer.'

'I think you'll find it much more economical,' Dugald supplemented.

Victoria flushed with annoyance. Once more coals of fire were being shovelled. 'It's very kind of you, but I'm not sure . . .'

'Miss Elliott, if I might make a suggestion.' Suavity did not quite conceal the speaker's impatience. 'We have a quorum. Let sleeping sisters lie. The wean has no liking for me. She would as lief starve her dogs as accept favours from the enemy.'

'Very funny!' Victoria clipped.

'Very charming,' he returned gallantly, looking from T-strap sandals to full skirt and a glimpse of suntanned shoulders. 'Too much so to die in battle.'

An unfair chemistry made her blush. 'Do you patronise everyone, or is it just me?'

'Patronise?' He looked astonished. 'No, Miss Elliott, there's a more efficacious treatment in store for you.' Before she could guess his intention he bent forward and kissed her full and firmly on the mouth.

As she stood gasping, he swung himself back in the saddle. 'And another time don't open your mouth so provocatively, or I might have to shut it again!'

A touch sent the grey cantering down the glen.

Lorraine's happy mood was evident. As she got ready for bed Victoria could hear her singing:

' "He had laughed on the lass with his bonny black eye." '

It was ironic. Lorraine had a pretty voice and she

79

used it unselfconsciously. She had lilted like a lark on what would have been her wedding morning, but not since. And now it had to be for Dugald Douglas.

When Victoria went downstairs next morning, the breakfast table was laid and the coffee perking. Lorraine was wearing a dress instead of trousers and she looked radiant. The visit to Baldougrie had been most enjoyable and she had met Dugald's two young assistants. Victoria asked if there had been any sign of the missing partner, M. McAlaster, but Lorraine said no. Dugald, she volunteered, had a musical side to him. They had had a singalong and he had taught her Allen-a-Dale.

'So I heard last night,' Victoria said, passing the marmalade. 'I thought you'd discovered Scott, seemingly it's only Douglas!'

'I like the *song*,' Lorraine stated with a blush. 'And the setting. He did that himself from a traditional melody.'

She sang a line or two.

' "Allen-a-Dale is not baron or lord
    Yet twenty strong yeomen will draw at his word." '

It would have been an appropriate signature tune for Dugald Douglas himself.

Victoria, elbows resting on the table, had been waiting a chance to speak. Suddenly she couldn't—at least not in the way she had intended.

'Lorrie, you should know something. I found it out by chance. He's had a tragedy in his life, similar to but more final than yours. He's unlikely to involve himself again or to want promises. And there's another thing; up to three years ago he was in Naval Intelligence. Given certain contingencies, I imagine he could take any personality that suited the need.' As silence fell she wished she need not have spoken. 'You know, I suspect him of bringing about Aunt Elizabeth's trauma.'

'I know that's ridiculous.' Lorraine had got her voice back. A spot of colour flamed on each cheekbone. 'So is the other thing. All of it. If you're implying ...'

'I'm not.' Victoria's protest was drowned in a volley of barking from the garden. Hairylegs and the boarder were beside themselves with excitement. Investigation showed a cat on the roof. Lorraine grabbed Hairylegs and bore him off kicking. Victoria shut the boarder in one of the sheds.

There remained the cat standing on the ridge like a weather vane. Behind it, the sky was now a dazzling blue and the disc round its neck glinted in the sun.

'If I had a ladder ...' Victoria thought aloud.

'No,' said Lorraine flatly. 'No. Period. Oh, look, Vic, finish your breakfast. You know we said we'd go to church this morning.'

Victoria had a feeling they were being watched. She turned round sharply, but the road was empty and across it the trees in the wood were motionless. She frowned and walked to the gate. Immediately a boy stepped from behind a beech tree and came forward.

He looked about twelve, slim and fair with a critical expression. If he had ever soiled his hands or been in a rugby scrum it didn't show.

'If I might make a suggestion,' he said confidently. 'The law of gravity ensures that what goes up must come down.'

Victoria wondered if she had heard aright. The boy's striking dark eyes, however, were profoundly serious. She said hastily: 'Quite so. Why didn't I think of that?'

'I don't know,' he told her simply.

On impulse she introduced herself. Her visitor did not follow suit. He smiled and walked away from her down the road.

'I've met precocious children,' Victoria declared to Lorraine. 'But that one wasn't believable.'

It was difficult to slot him into the village. In the midst of pondering his origins they realised that there was a cat on the grass outside the window, a striped cat wearing a blue collar with a dangling silver disc.

'That's *it*!' Victoria breathed. 'Three cheers for the law of gravity!'

It should have ended the matter. The cat, back on *terra firma*, should have gone home. It didn't. It strolled into the kitchen and ordered breakfast. It had a surname—Bradley—and a telephone number. It also had an appetite.

'It has been here before,' Lorraine said resignedly. 'Good thing we can send it home.'

'I wouldn't bank on that.' Victoria had been studying the cat's disc. 'This isn't a local number.'

She dialled and discovered that the Bradleys lived near Leeds but had a holiday home in Strathfin. During a recent stay in it, the cat had gone missing. Mrs Bradley was overjoyed to hear that her pet was safe but not at all surprised to learn where it had turned up. 'They all get in on the act, don't they?' she chuckled. 'Your great-aunt ruined every animal within miles.'

In the end it was arranged that the Bradley cat should room at the refuge until next weekend when his owners could claim him. Victoria disclaimed thanks and went to break the news to Lorraine. Her sister, however, had taken the car out and was waiting with a somewhat long-suffering air.

The post and lantern, noticed previously, marked the path to the kirk. As simple as their first visit had shown, its lancet windows were mostly plain glass; in the east end there was just one small light of the Good Shepherd.

Victoria looking about for the mystery boy accepted that he was not present. Across the aisle Craig Maxwell caught her eye and from some distance behind him Ellen Fenwick beamed. On the right was a miniature transept containing three pews. A scrutiny of the memorial tablets which overshadowed them showed that these were the castle pews. Victoria read the name of Walter Douglas and the names of his parents. A third tablet commemorated a Captain Douglas who had served in the Cameronians.

She let her eyes drop from the memorial and was annoyed with herself for starting. She had not seen Dugald come in.

Dress was Victoria's living; it was also a many-splendoured thing. National dress came into this category.

Dugald, walking to the lectern to perform his accustomed duty as laird, was an object lesson. The tweed kilt jacket, which today replaced the working battle dress blouse, was fawn and threw up the lovely greens and blues of the tartan. She noted the scarlet tabs on the natural spun kilt hose and the *sgian dubh* in the top of the right stocking.

Then to her mortification he lifted his eyes from the Bible. The moment had a terrifying alchemy. For a second it made her forget Aunt Elizabeth. She smiled shyly, blushed and looked away.

The Minister prefaced his sermon by a word on a local matter, the cause of much concern. Sheep worrying. Normally prevalent in the spring when lambs were young, this year had seen it reach a peak and persist. The local farmers, some of whom had lost half their flock in a night, had now organised patrols to keep watch on the sheep. He appealed to all dog-owners in his congregation to make sure their pets were indoors at night. No matter how small and apparently docile, a dog changed its character when it ran with a pack at dark. He gave details, for which he apologised, of the *modus operandi* and the injuries inflicted. This done, he gave out his text.

The sermon came a poor second to the speech which had preceded it. Sheep worrying had always caused Victoria a shudder, but in London it had been remote. Up here she was living in the midst of the trouble. In front of her the Good Shepherd window took on new relevance.

# CHAPTER SIX

A few days passed. They bought a pack of dog meat which Lorraine cooked and took up to Ellen for storage in the Baldougrie freezer. No more waifs and strays had turned up and life was becoming more organised.

They had not seen Dugald since Sunday. In fact the only visitors to Wild Heart were the Minister and the fair-headed boy who still chose to remain anonymous. Victoria found him prowling round the premises as though he owned them.

'What do you do with your eggs?' he asked inquisitively.

'What does one usually do with eggs?' she returned, nettled.

Not a spasm crossed the round face. The boy was better looking than most, questioning black eyes, straight honey-coloured hair and a slim neck.

'One usually sells them, I would have thought,' he answered politely. 'You could put up a notice "Fresh Farm Eggs".'

'Only that it doesn't happen to be a farm.'

The boy let this pass since he was now preoccupied with the bolts on the hen-house. 'These are out of true. In fact all your bolts should be re-fitted.'

'In time,' Victoria said shortly.

He was gently firm. 'It would be quite easy for an animal to open these doors.'

'It wouldn't be so easy for a *hen*.' She was determined to have the last word.

The boy left her and went sauntering down the glen.

She thought of him with some discomfiture the next day when Hairylegs and the boarding dog were sighted on the far side of the gate. I can't have pushed the bolt far enough, she thought. It would be something to watch in future.

Craig had explained that she should attend his clinic whether or not she had any patients to bring. The Welfare Society who financed his services had looked upon Aunt Elizabeth as a link man.

He had not been specific on what would be required of her, but Victoria had thought vaguely that she might preside over the Society's collecting box. In fact there was a lot to do. She found he was depending on her to show folk into the surgery and in some cases to hold the patients. Child owners were not admitted unless accompanied by an adult and Craig was so pushed for time that he could not spare even the seconds necessary to learn an animal's name.

'Sorry, Victoria, but we don't chat them up. We'd be here till doomsday if we did. You'll learn.'

She hoped so; she was ashamed of her lack of skill. Cats that had looked dozy with their mistresses became more like tigers when set on the table for examination. Time and again they lurched out of her grasp. 'Can you keep them steady?' Craig requested temperately. 'We'll know all about it if the syringe meets the wrong organ.'

Nothing untoward occurred and they finished in good time. 'Just what I was aiming for,' Craig said with satisfaction. 'Jim Redfern is waiting for us in the Horse. I told him we wouldn't be late.'

It was good of him to have remembered this contact of Aunt Elizabeth's. Victoria, duly ensconced at a table under a beam hung with copper jugs, was grateful. In practical terms, however, it was disappointing. Jim Redfern knew no more than she did herself about her aunt's routine.

'Not to worry,' he said comfortingly. 'You can play it by ear.'

The *Argus*, he added, naming the paper for which he worked, would give her full support.

In the way of placing the homeless this would be invaluable, and Victoria stifled her previous disappointment and thanked him warmly. Since there was no information to acquire, she would have preferred to get home, but neither Craig nor Jim Redfern would hear of it.

'My turn now,' the journalist insisted. 'What about you, Vic? Same again?'

The abbreviation of her name was a little surprising, but then Jim's world did not stand on ceremony.

At the same moment the door behind them opened. Victoria saw the landlord look towards the entrant with esteem. He said warmly: 'Good evening, Mr Douglas.'

It was absurd, but as in the kirk on Sunday she felt herself flush with embarrassment. Idiotic and infuriating. Dugald had kissed her, yes, half joke, half insult. Like his ancestors who had tweaked English noses all along the Border. It was said that inter-marriage had made Clan Douglas more royal than the Sovereign.

This Douglas, she realised, was angry. Steel blue eyes whipped round the bar and settled on Craig. 'I thought your time was seven till eight. Have you changed it? There are folk standing waiting at your door.'

Craig flicked a glance at his wrist. 'They're out of luck, then. We had to put our skates on tonight. Victoria wanted to meet Jim.'

No one could dispute the truth of it, the implication made Victoria squirm. She shifted wretchedly, feeling like a criminal. Dugald's stony gaze did not shift at all.

'Yes, well, it's none of my business,' he said shortly. 'But I think a word of explanation wouldn't come amiss. I'm looking for Ellen. I dropped her and said I'd come back.'

Ellen had indeed been at the clinic with her black and white cat who was having a course of injections. Obviously the early closing had left her with no place where she could wait. The cat, Victoria recalled, had been large and heavy.

'Why didn't she say?' she exclaimed impulsively. 'We could have let her stay.'

'You don't know Ellen.' Dugald's face relaxed for a second. 'Where she comes from they don't ask favours. It's no great matter. I'll catch her on the road.'

The landlord offered him a drink. He declined it courteously but hurriedly and was gone.

'Nice friendly feller,' Jim Redfern remarked humorously.

Craig muttered something and drained his glass. Victoria sat silent, realising that she could not totally absolve herself. She had been under strain and too relieved to question it when he'd said they were through.

'Cheer up,' Craig said rallyingly. 'It's not your fault. I've a clock that goes fast, that's all, and I didn't think of it.' As she shook her head, he made a playful moue. 'What did I call you two the first day we met? Conscience and Conscience's Keeper. It seems I was right. So what do we do now? Go back and see who is waiting?'

'I'd feel a lot happier.'

'So be it,' he said indulgently.

By this time, however, everyone had given up and gone home.

'Let this be a lesson to you,' Craig teased. 'Keep your eye on me! Your aunt never let me away with anything.' The twinkle was infectious. She had to smile at it. 'Back at the ranch,' Craig joked. 'We have a drink to finish.'

A few days later, Mrs Bradley from Leeds claimed her 'happy wanderer' with a generous donation towards the expenses of the refuge. It transpired that the Bradley holiday home was the next house round the elbow with an unimpeded view of the controversial Wild Heart hutches.

'As a matter of fact, my husband had words with Miss Elliott about it,' Mrs Bradley admitted. 'Quite unsuccessfully. She was a very formidable lady. She threw him out!'

The dogs' walk before supper was always a pleasant duty. That evening they went round the elbow past the beautiful closed gates of the castle. Victoria found these a constant enigma.

'I expect they'll open them when a Stewart comes to the throne,' she surmised lightly. 'I did ask Ellen, but she wouldn't say.'

'Ellen never says anything, you should know that by now,' Lorraine responded. 'Try asking Dugald.'

'Dugald and I don't have that kind of relationship, *you* should know that!' Victoria retorted. She could still see his look of displeasure in the Grey Horse and felt no doubt that she had been the prime target. No matter what shadings of blame might exist, it was evident that in Dugald's mind she was exactly what he had thought at first, lightweight and irresponsible.

On the way home they passed the Bradley home, a well planned bungalow which must have cost a great deal. Simultaneously they both slowed down. There was no doubt about it. Looking across the glen, Aunt Elizabeth's buildings stuck out like a sore thumb.

'Are *you* thinking what I'm thinking?' Lorraine suggested suddenly. 'Mr Bradley put a lot of money into this place, and a lot of thought, she said they'd been looking for years before they bought it. Would you blame him if he complained to the Council?'

When Victoria woke next morning she felt that a consoling thought was just out of reach.

The newsagent's schoolboy son had stuck the paper in the letter box and she went to retrieve it. Two papers, she realised in surprise. One was their usual daily, the other a complimentary copy of the *Argus*, which came out on Saturdays. She took them and went to the kitchen. The red kitten had already called up to her that it was time for breakfast. She opened the door and it did its jelly roll on the floor.

Of all the animals, Victoria had a special love for the kitten. Tango, as she had named it, was the mascot of Wild Heart and kept the whole place under surveillance.

Unfortunately Lorraine did not seem to be stirring. A headache, she admitted ruefully, when Victoria put her head round the door. It was not a bad one and she had been remarkably free of them since coming to Strathfin.

'Thanks. That's marvellous,' she said gratefully, sipping the tea Victoria had brought. 'Just give me an hour or two and I'll be fine.'

There was just one thing. She remembered it as Victoria got to the door. Dog meat had to be fetched from Baldougrie that morning, and soon, so that it would de-freeze.

Victoria took the *Argus* to read while she was having breakfast. As she unfolded it, her jaw dropped. The last thing she had expected was to find Wild Heart on the front page. But there it was—a photograph of the house and the notice-board, and a headline: VICTORIA IS NOT AMUSED. Astounded, she read on.

'Strathfin is proud to welcome a celebrity to its ranks. Victoria Elliott, well known in the world of fashion, has become the new champion of the underdog—and cat. Victoria was in fighting form when I talked to her after the weekly clinic initiated through the efforts of her indomitable great-aunt. "Aunt Elizabeth died for what she believed in," she told me with a toss of a very determined chin. "They won't find me so easy to kill." '

There was more in like vein. Victoria read it in a daze. It was badly written, extravagant, largely unverified. Jib Redfern had given her no idea of his intentions. Above all, however, it made her laugh.

In many places it had been a 'scorched earth' summer, but trees kept Baldougrie green. This morning its sweeps of emerald turf were dotted with the black and chamois forms of Labradors at field training.

Victoria could not but admit that it was a scene after her own heart. She had stayed aloof only because she had been certain it was enemy territory. This morning, for the first time, she had an alternative suspect—Mr Bradley. Lorraine's theory was convincing and didn't stop there. She wished it could be true. They didn't know Mr Bradley, there were no complications like storing dog meat and shutting up the hens.

'I could have been wrong about Dugald.' Victoria had her waking up thought in the open at last. It was like losing a burden.

The Number Seven was a happy dog—with good eyesight. He recognised her even from a distance and came at full tilt with his mouth open. Victoria stopped, flushing with embarrassment, but it was too late. On came the Number Seven, all concentration shattered. Behind him came Dugald with an inscrutable face. Knees under the apron of a kilt have an aggressive look.

She faltered an apology. 'Sorry. I seem to have distracted him. I shouldn't have come this way.'

'If you wanted me you had no option.' He looked down at her with the ghost of a twinkle.

The ensuing half hour was engrossing. The dogs had been divided into three groups; one of Dugald's assistants had taken his detachment to the lake where they were learning water retrieves, the second assistant had the beginners working on land with the wooden dummies Victoria had seen before. Dugald's group had progressed to feather training.

She was glad to see that the Number Seven had regained his place on the promotion ladder. Dugald gave the command to sit and then tossed something which looked like a stuffed pigeon on to the ground twenty-five yards in front of him. He shouted: 'Fetch!' and Number Seven obeyed.

'Training them must be difficult,' Victoria observed.

'In varying degrees.' His hand stayed on Number Seven's head. 'But rewarding and essential to well-being.'

'You must find it a change from the services,' she ventured.

'Yes, but complementary. I don't think I'd discipline animals if I hadn't first taken it myself.'

It was a humbling instance of how prepared Dugald was for the task he had inherited. She, by contrast, had jumped into hers with both feet. And yet he had not spoken unkindly. Rather the reverse. 'The last time you came up here you wouldn't wait for coffee. Can we repair that deficiency?'

'If you're sure it won't delay you.'

'It will be my pleasure,' he said gently.

They crossed the lawn and went up a short flight of steps. A panorama of balustrades, terrace, and white squared glass stretched away to the right. The sun shone on cream curtain linings. These days the great rooms of Baldougrie were seldom in use.

Dugald brought her to a small, eminently lived-in room. There was a pipe on the mantelpiece, magazines on the table and a salmon rod in one corner. The morning papers, as yet unfolded, lay on a chair.

'Those pigeons the dogs were working with were alive,' Victoria said awkwardly.

'And stayed so. That was the object of the exercise.' He interpreted her thoughts. 'They're from a loft and used to being handled.' It was another stage in the emergence of a fully trained gun dog. The manner in which it mouthed a bird was all-important, ideally not a feather should be misplaced.

'Do you ever have casualties?' Victoria asked.

She was a little puzzled by his look. 'They're not unknown, but seldom the fault of the home team. Two marauders came up from the glen a few days ago and made away with one of the birds.' They had been spotted, he added, but unfortunately not in time.

'Could they have been the dogs who are after the sheep?' Victoria asked sympathetically.

His answer: 'I certainly hope not,' was a little surprising. So was the next question. 'What about Wild Heart? Everything under control?'

'Yes, fine,' she answered carelessly as Ellen brought in the tray. 'I've got the hang of it. No problems, really.'

'With small numbers, of course,' he qualified. 'You'd be well advised to keep it that way.'

Ellen's coffee predictably was very good, her shortbread petticoat tails delicious. Victoria was ashamed of her appetite. 'Lordy, no, I couldn't!' She had already had four. Nothing easier than to take a mouth-watering fifth, but there were limits.

Dugald did not recognise them. 'To please me?' His smile was lopsided and full of charm.

In a confusing way it won. 'Well, all right—if you put it like that!' Being pampered was a luxury not often afforded her. The shortbread reminded her of the kind Aunt Elizabeth used to send them for Christmas, long ago when Lorraine and she had been 'tiddlers'. Always the same round tin with the picture of Bonny Prince Charlie and always the lion's share for Lorrie and herself. This was the same sort of kindness.

To her own surprise she found herself talking about it, and the tricks their father used to play on them, hiding the tin, threatening to eat all the shortbread himself. 'It's quite silly, but just for the moment you reminded me of him.'

'I think I'm honoured,' Dugald said gravely. 'You were obviously very great with each other.'

The Scots phrase was satisfying. She had never admitted it, but she had always felt her father *had* thought her great—perhaps a tiny bit greater than Lorrie, who was so close to their mother.

'Yes, I think we were,' she said slowly. 'I was a greedy kid. When he petted me I lapped it up. I once wrote on his birthday present "From Victoria only" in case he'd think Lorrie had any part in it. Revolting, wasn't it?'

'No, not revolting. Frank. And telling. I hope——' He paused, his deep eyes very kind. 'I hope when you lost him, Victoria, there were other people ready to feed you shortbread biscuits.'

'Not really. But then I probably never gave them the chance. No, that's not true either. It was more—busyness. I'd a lot of growing up to do, no time for anything else.'

'Yes, I can see that,' he answered slowly. 'But there should always be time, Victoria, even if you can't have the right person.'

Her heart missed a beat. She knew they were talking not only of a tough little girl who had deliberately shut out sentiment, but of a man whom fate had robbed so cruelly. Dugald broke the silence.

'Perhaps we're getting too serious. Impel yourself to that last biscuit while I see what headlines we've made.' He took up the *Argus* and opened it. On the instant his face changed. When he lowered the sheet and looked at her he was grey with anger. 'What piece of lunacy is this?'

'Take it with a pinch of salt!' she said quickly.

'You authorised it?'

'I suppose so.' None knew better than she did that ethics had not been observed. On the other hand, Jim Redfern had undoubtedly felt he could count on her.

'You're a foolish girl,' Dugald said quietly. 'You've let Redfern take you, and unless we move fast you'll reap the consequences.' He tapped the offending column. 'What you've let him print may be actionable, I don't know. I do know that six animals are too much for you; what will you do with sixty?'

Victoria had a glimmer of understanding. 'Sixty is rubbish.'

'Not so.' His calmness made it more sinister. 'This is an invitation. With attractive bait. They'll come. Redfern will get his story and you'll get the debris. Sixty is no wild vision, I wish it were.'

It was like arguing with a rock. But Victoria was the terrier breed. Dugald had just stated that there was a week before the *Argus* could publish a retraction, in the meantime they must put the word around that Wild Heart was not geared for an invasion. 'Fortunately, we can do it in a place this size; my lads will help —and Ellen. She can talk when she has a mind to.' There might have been a twinkle, but Victoria refused to see it.

'I keep telling you. I'm not retracting. This is what Wild Heart is for.'

'A jumped-up scoop for the newspapers?' He picked her scathingly. 'Your aunt and I had our differences,

95

but I never underestimated her intelligence. She would have sent him packing.'

'I beg to disagree. Craig told me they were good friends.'

'Oh, lassie!' Dugald said wearily. 'Must you always take the opposite view?'

'It seems I have no option.' She spoke with a queer kind of sadness.

The death of their shortlived friendship was no surprise. It had had as much chance as a match flame. She looked at Dugald standing at the window and noted the broad dark back to his head.

'You must understand,' he said heavily. 'I do not wish to see you disadvantaged or the glen in chaos. It's in your make-up to bring both these to pass.'

Something seemed to snap in Victoria's brain. 'The first is not your business! And the second—I imagine your chief concern—is not at issue. We look after our animals, you know that.'

'I know that your dogs get out. They were up here two days ago. They killed that pigeon.'

It was a douche of cold water. She remembered the day they had seen Hairylegs and the other dog frolicking in the field. 'I'm sorry. We had no idea. You must let me pay for the damage.'

'I didn't say it with that intention.' He turned round.

'You said it to gloat.' She was being crude, but she couldn't help it. 'I know what you think of me. It's in my make-up to make a mess of things. That's what you thought the first day we met and you've just said it again. It's a war of nerves, isn't it? You're trying to drive me out ...'

'And you're being very blind.' Dugald had gripped her arm. The pressure of his fingers was warm and strangely personal. Her hand started to tremble.

'What is it? Why are you staring at me?' If she didn't

96

stop him he would see the dreams of years, the loneliness and the heartache.

'I was thinking about a day in the Highlands when I went out with my brother-in-law to get a wild cat that was after his game. When we caught up with it, it was a young one, thick-coated, brindled, eyes like wild topaz. I saw that creature blaze with hatred when it spotted us, and I've never forgotten how beautiful it was.' He paused.

Victoria could see the wild cat and feel the despair of its losing battle.

'But you *killed* it,' she accused. 'What mattered to the cat was life. It didn't care what you thought of it, any more than I do. That's whitewash like ...' Biting the words back, she realised what she had been about to say: 'That's whitewash like the odd sop you throw to my aunt's memory.'

'Yes?' he prompted.

She said hastily, 'It doesn't matter. I must go.'

Dugald beckoned from the window and one of his young assistants appeared.

'Victoria wants a word with Gibson about locks and bolts. Show her where to find him. I'm pushed for time.' He went to the door and stopped. 'By the way, I didn't finish my story. The cat was too good for us. She got away.'

# CHAPTER SEVEN

SANDY GIBSON, the village locksmith, promised to go up to Wild Heart after the weekend. Victoria tried to wring a definite promise for Monday, but was not hopeful.

When she got within sight of home she saw incredulously that there were people on the doorstep. A dog and a pregnant cat were seeking admission. Before the day was over, more had arrived, and Victoria suspected uneasily that curiosity did indeed lie at the root of it.

'Tell them we can't take any more,' Lorraine commanded when the count reached a staggering eighteen.

'There's no use talking like that,' Victoria retorted. 'We're supposed to be running a refuge. Aunt Elizabeth had up to fifty cats at one time.'

'Then it's no wonder someone complained about her.' Lorraine had been appalled to hear the dogs had trespassed. She harped on it for most of the day.

On Sunday morning Victoria found one of the new cats with an eye closed. By now she knew enough to be anxious. It could be the start of 'flu.

'Can *we* catch it?' Lorraine asked apprehensively.

'No, but you'd better keep away. I'll take it down to Craig.'

She rang the vet's doorbell about eleven, embarrassingly near the kirk and its arriving congregation. There was some delay before the ring was answered and Craig appeared in a short pale blue robe.

'For heaven's sake, you eager beaver,' he said with amusement. 'This is Sunday!'

'I'm sorry, my darling, I'm not really at home today,'

he added when she had explained her call. 'I've got a friend with me. If you like to leave it till later and give me a ring.'

Victoria felt abashed. Admittedly, she had panicked.

'Not to worry,' Craig smiled indulgently. 'I gather business is booming.'

He listened goodhumouredly, leaning against the door post and looking long-legged and biscuit colour. 'Sorry about this. Ring me if you're still worried.' He followed her to the car and waved after it. 'See you!'

It was a relief that he was not embarrassed. Victoria felt an idiot as she drove away.

The fair-headed boy was talking to Lorraine in the garden.

'Hello,' Victoria greeted him briskly. 'I'm beginning to think you're related to the Cheshire Cat. It's the way you come and go.'

'I'm sorry. I don't know what you mean,' he said politely.

She stared. '*Alice in Wonderland*. The Cheshire Cat.'

'I don't believe I've read it.'

Victoria looked at the serious face and decided it was not a leg-pull. Not for the first time she wondered about the parents of this unchildlike child.

'Yes. Well, never mind. We should all be in the kirk, of course, but as we're not let's go and have some lemonade. It's about all we've got left in the house!'

The lemonade went some way towards breaking the ice. Names were exchanged. The boy's was Magnus, he did not volunteer the rest of it.

'As to church,' he added casually. 'I don't go. I've lost my faith.'

The purpose of his call at Wild Heart today was to warn them that there was a fox in the vicinity. He had seen it himself that morning crossing the road further down the glen.

'Do you live near?' Victoria asked curiously.

He was not the chatty type and now he merely glanced at her. 'That's right.'

'What an extraordinary child,' Lorraine commented after he had gone.

'I rather like him,' Victoria admitted. 'I think he could grow on me.'

During the evening they had a surprise visitor— Craig, fully clothed and bearing a bottle of wine.

'*Mea culpa*. Peace-offering,' he said handing it over.

'For the cat?' Victoria blushed at the memory. 'You don't need to apologise. I should have had more sense.'

He flashed her a grin and they both laughed. The cat, however, was not the point at issue. Victoria could see he had almost forgotten it.

'Is there another sin we should know about?' she joked.

'You do already. Your strong-arm man gave Jim his first taste of the protection racket.' Craig was still smiling, but the smile was skin-deep.

'I don't follow,' Victoria began uneasily.

'Then I'd better spell it out as he did. "Hands off Wild Heart. It's mine."' Dugald Douglas, he went on, had gone into the office of the *Argus* in the next town and had given Jim Redfern a rough time.

'He didn't go on my authority. He had no right!' Victoria was justly angry. Once more she had been treated like a child. Was there no end to the arrogance of this self-styled clan chief?

But that was exactly what Craig was saying and even humorously accepting. He reminded her lightly of the days when the Douglas family had been the protectors of all those who took the clan name.

'Which doesn't apply to anyone in this house!' Victoria retorted. 'And I do think it's carrying his interest in the property a bit far.'

'You're not being fair to him, Vic.' Lorraine's cheeks had gone pink. 'He's right—we are in a mess.'

'Which I admit is partly my fault.' Craig ceased laughing. 'So for a start let me see this cat and any others you may be worried about.'

He fetched his case from the car and set to work examining eyes and looking down throats. There was nothing seriously wrong.

'You know, you've done a good job,' he said warmly. 'This place used to look like a shambles.'

'My aunt was old and ill,' Victoria countered sharply.

Nevertheless his praise was welcome. They had both worked hard, clearing out and tidying. She had given the hutches a coat of paint, cut the grass plot and cleaned the windows. Lorraine had washed all the curtains. Plenty of elbow grease had gone into the past couple of weeks, but there were still many needs, some large like new fencing and doors, some small like food and water bowls, collars and leads and sleeping baskets.

'Don't sentimentalise,' Craig warned. 'They're not permanencies, you know. Take them in and then get them out as fast as you can. That kitten, for instance, it's a healthy little beast and people go for that colour. I'll find you a home for it.' He was looking, Victoria realised, at Tango draped along a shelf, his swansdown paws hanging like ballet shoes.

'Oh!' Her heart missed a beat. 'Well, he's a bit special, Craig. I call him the mascot.'

'And I could call you a soggy sentimentalist!' Craig said teasingly. 'But I won't. When are you coming out with me again?'

It was impossible not to like him. He was so ready to answer for his faults and to make amends. True, he might not be the traditional country vet, but that alone was refreshing.

Next day it was no surprise that the locksmith did

not turn up. Victoria went to his cottage and was told he was away for the day. She did not believe it, but was powerless. There was nothing for it but to patch up the barricades herself. It took four laborious hours and a bruised thumb, but it was essential for peace of mind.

'Oh, Vic, leave it. It's a job for a man,' Lorraine demurred. In the end, however, she lent a hand, something the old Lorraine would never have attempted.

All in all, both of them had earned their night's rest, but, as luck would have it, when bedtime came Hairy-legs refused to settle. It was unusual; he was a little dog who liked his comforts and he had always been more than happy to sleep in Lorraine's room. Tonight he behaved like a demon, barking, whining and scratching at the back door.

'He wants to sleep outside with the others.' Lorraine was a little put out.

They now had two dogs in addition to the terrier they were boarding for the children. One stray, grey-muzzled and stiff, was too old to give trouble; the other was large and not particularly friendly. Hairylegs loved them all.

When Victoria took him out to join them in the pen excitement was intense.

All I want for Christmas is a pair of ear-plugs, she thought ruefully as the uproar wafted up through the bedroom window.

It eased after a while, but somehow she found herself lying awake, her thoughts dwelling on Lorrie working at the fence. Her sister was becoming quite an outdoor girl, and how quickly she reacted to criticism of Dugald.

'Oh dear,' Victoria thought. 'I do hope she hasn't fallen for him.'

The moon was shining full on the bed and she got up to draw the curtains. Outside was a silver landscape, closed gates, the shape of old Charlie the gelding under his tree and—great grief! her heart turned over—the forms of three dogs scampering into the distance.

'Not ours,' Victoria half prayed, half cried as she ran downstairs. 'Not after all that work!'

The silence was answer enough. Not a bark as she opened the door. The pen's sole occupant, old Grey Beard, opened an eye and shut it again. What stung most was that, having burst open the door of their pen, the escapees had made such short work of her job on the perimeter fence. The chain link fencing was tough, but determined bodies had made a bulge in it. Quite a small bulge. How the big dog had got through it was a mystery. Needs must, she supposed, when the devil drove. The thought was sickeningly apt. Hairylegs's frenzy in the kitchen had been abnormal.

And if the devil *were* driving, the question was: 'Where to?'

Five minutes later, Victoria's cotton nightgown was lying in a ball on the bed. Victoria, small and tousle-headed in jeans and sweater, was racing across Charlie's field.

Baldougrie was the first place she thought of. She went up the brae as best she could, clutching at roots to steady herself. The dreaded words rang all the time in her head; when Mr Black had used them in the kirk a week ago they had seemed scaring, now they were terrifying. 'Something gets into a dog when he runs with a pack at dark.'

The climb was almost worth the effect when she scrambled the last few yards over the rim of the glen and saw the castle and its Gothic towers by moonlight. The dogs, however, did not materialise; the thing she shrank from did. Faint and faraway—the bleating of sheep.

Judging from the weakness of the sound, she had a

long way to go. The Douglas family had long since sold the home farm and all the tenant farms on the estate, but the castle was still the focal point in a radius of several miles. Victoria never lost sight of it nor it of her.

Her wind and her legs were beginning to give out as she stopped gasping in the middle of the moor. And then suddenly she saw the field below her.

It was bathed in moonlight, a bright relief against the moorland slopes that surrounded it. The wretched sheep and their lambs—Victoria caught her breath in anguish—had huddled together at one end, their bleating heartrendingly human. The dogs were dashing about, Hairylegs yapping with joy.

'Oh, God!' Victoria exclaimed without irreverence.

The nightmare would happen before her eyes. The crazed sheep would be picked out and driven into the brambles to a horrible death. 'They can literally eat them alive,' Mr Black had said.

'No! No! Hairylegs! Stop it! Come back!' Victoria shouted, plunging down the slope.

What happened next was confusion. Victoria stopped only to snatch up a dead branch. She brandished it wildly from side to side. The black dog ignored her, the children's white terrier ran away and miraculously Hairylegs stopped for a second and she seized him. Holding him was quite a feat. He went mad in her arms. As she hung on grimly she felt his teeth in her hand.

She could not have told how long she had been struggling before her ears caught a new sound—a long low whistle perforating the clamour of the dogs. She looked up and for the moment froze with fear. A man was standing on the slope. At first glance he was unfamiliar, rough dark hair, thick homespun sweater, dark trousers. He was carrying a rifle.

Her head spun as he came towards her, but flight was

instinctive. She started to run, felt herself grabbed and stopped. In the same instant an arm went round her, pulling her close.

'Quiet!' warned a voice in her ear. 'Do as I say.'

Victoria jerked her head incredulously and saw that the arm holding her was Dugald's.

The leap her heart gave contradicted all reason. Clear and primitive the thought came: I don't have to worry. Dugald will know what to do.

She was right. Dugald acted swiftly. He laid down the rifle and took Hairylegs.

'I've a patrol on my tail. It's best they shouldn't see you.'

Victoria did not question. He hurried her up the slope to a crevice in the rock and still silently she edged in out of sight. In the kirk that Sunday Mr Black had mentioned the vigilante patrols which the local farmers were organising. To be caught in the act by one of those would mean curtains for the dog concerned.

Extraordinarily it seemed that Hairylegs was to be given a second chance. Dugald's hands, working like lightning, bound a handkerchief round the dog's wet muzzle and fastened the lead which Victoria had been vainly trying to engage. She looped it over her wrist.

'If you lose him he's for it.' The whisper was decisive.

'I won't,' she mouthed, shaking her head.

His eye fell suddenly on her hand and he frowned and lifted it to examine the toothmarks it bore. For a second their eyes met. Then he pressed a hand on her shoulder and was gone.

She risked a peep from her hiding place and saw that he had gone down the slope again and retrieved the rifle. Then running feet and shouts from the rest of the patrol sent her squeezing back against the wall of the fissure.

Why had he done it? Hairylegs, unlike the Number Seven, was no pedigree Labrador with money tied up in him. It would have seemed like asking the impossible to expect Dugald to see Hairylegs as she did, a silly stumpy little dog who had been the first to make friends.

Yet this was the miracle that had happened, that and the strange comfort his eyes had sent her.

The wait was uneventful but nerve-racking. The sounds from outside told her what was happening and she had heard a shot. But presently the last of the piteous bleating died away.

The men's voices drew nearer, talking soberly but with satisfaction. One rose above the others: 'Och, Dugald, where's your hurry? Will you no' come back for a dram?'

'Ay indeed. It's yourself has earned it,' another chimed in.

'Another time,' Dugald's voice answered. 'If you'll excuse me now I'm away to my bed. I've an early start in the morning.'

Goodnights were called and she heard footsteps crunching through the scree and coming nearer. Dugald eased into the crevice and let himself down beside her.

'Are you all right, lass? You worried me that time.'

It was aeons removed from the tirade she had expected. She asked warily: 'Can I talk?' and saw his amusement as he nodded.

'I should be concerned to think you had lost the power of speech.'

'I have to thank you for what you did.' Now that the tension had abated she felt almost shy of him. 'Dugald' meant 'Dark Stranger', and never had it been more apt than at the moment when he had seemed to come from nowhere and she had failed to recognise him.

'There was no need for a holocaust,' he said briefly. 'I knew Pedro was not the culprit.' She had looked surprised and he added: 'It is your aunt's dog, isn't it? The one she called Pedro?'

It was a little like discovering that Hairylegs had a new identity. 'It's a rather grander name than I gave him,' Victoria confessed. 'Hairylegs.'

'Hairylegs?' The shaky light showed Dugald's face was twitching. He straightened it. 'Yes, I see what you mean.'

She wondered if she was dreaming the tenderness in his eyes.

'Do you know what happened?' she asked painfully. 'If the sheep were injured I must accept responsibility.'

'The sheep were upset, no more. And it's unlikely to recur. The black dog was the one we've been looking for. He has killed his last sheep in the glen.'

Somehow she did not need to ask who had fired the shot.

But the strain was telling at last. Tears that she was hardly aware of sprang to her eyes. It was all too much, she was tired, her hand was throbbing and she was sad, sad in a complicated way because she had never felt at home with the black dog. He had been a loser, a misfit whom she had not been able to help.

'Victoria?' Dugald was peering at her. 'Oh, my dear ...' Before she had time to realise his intention he had extracted a handkerchief and was drying her face. 'My dear, my dear,' he said gently. 'Don't distress yourself. You did well. I saw how brave you were, my little one. Don't cry. It had to be.'

It was surely part of the dream that as she stared at him wide-eyed he bent forward and kissed her cheek.

'And now we must get you to the doctor,' he said briskly. 'That hand must be seen to.'

Protests availed nothing.

'Oh no,' Victoria demurred. 'It hardly hurts at all.'

'Oh *yes*. You need an anti-tetanus injection,' he corrected calmly.

The walk back to Baldougrie, her hand through Dugald's arm, retained the dreamlike quality. Moonlight flung their shadows on the heath, Dugald's with the gun slung on his shoulder and Hairylegs' lead in his free hand. The little dog trotted along quietly all his passion spent.

Victoria fretted for the children's terrier who had apparently been too scared to show himself. Dugald said comfortingly that he would find his way home. By now he had heard the full story.

'I wish you'd let me know about Gibson. I'd have seen to it. I know his form.' The locksmith, he promised, would be there at crack of dawn.

Ahead of them Baldougrie glimmered in the moonlight, a ghost castle straight from *Marmion* or *The Lay of the Last Minstrel*. In this light the shadows on the high turrets could have been knights in armour and the arch into the courtyard could well have had a warder on guard above it. Then staghounds would have slept on the rush-strewn floor and all the chief's kinsmen would have hung their shields in the hall.

Tonight modern shields of skilfully beaten copper graced the rough-cast walls and the Number Seven stretched out on a Persian rug got up and came to meet them.

'At the risk of shattering your illusions,' Dugald said whimsically. 'We have hot and cold, and if you want to make use of them while I give the doctor a ring it's this way.' He conducted her to a spacious cloakroom.

Victoria was almost afraid to look in the glass. She was made of suggestible material and it was all wrong to come into a place like this in jeans and a sweater. Dugald's garb, casual though it was, was helped by his strong dark hair and the lines of thought on his face.

She was achingly conscious of how different she must look from the girl who should have been here to-day as the mistress of Baldougrie. Tonight that presence was an almost physical one. She saw a tall figure, dark silky hair, porcelain cheekbones, a long graceful skirt. 'Oh yes, she was *beautiful*,' those who knew her had said. 'I saw how brave you were, my little one,' was undoubtedly the consolation prize.

It took courage to face reality. She brushed down her dark blue jeans and straightened the cherry red sweater.

Dugald had told Dr Mackie that they would be along in half an hour.

'Didn't he mind? I'm sure he was in bed.'

'Doctors have been known to get up if a patient calls them,' he said drily.

The hall was full of good things. Oriel windows. A soft wall light blooming on a painting of a Cavalier. Muted golds and reds in the brocade curtains. A splash of blue and green from the tartan of a young officer in the Cameronians whose portrait hung above the hearth.

Dugald poured whisky from a beautiful old decanter. He brought two glasses across the room, put one firmly into her hand and raised the other with a brisk: '*Slainte.*'

'Now you *need* that,' he cautioned. 'Drink it up.'

'I'm afraid I'm a little bemused. I don't often do my drinking in such stateliness. Baldougrie is a Gaelic name, isn't it? What does it mean?'

'Literally—"The big house in the dark glen." ' It had been built by a famous architect for a wealthy Douglas in the last century. 'The last of the big spenders,' his descendant remarked. 'And you can probably see why.' The present castle had been raised on the site of a ruined one. 'We've been around this part of the Border for six hundred years. We were at Flodden, naturally, and some of my father's branch went to Killiecrankie with Claverhouse and brought back a snip off his blood-stained coat. Some day when we've more time I'll show it to you. It's been passed down from father to eldest son ever since. As a family we tend to go by the book.'

'And the book says the gates of the castle must always be kept closed?' Victoria could not resist the question.

'Failing certain conditions,' he agreed gravely.

'May I know them?'

The thought seemed to amuse him. He gave her a long quizzical look. 'That would be telling.'

'Answers to questions usually are.'

'A truism,' he conceded. 'But the time is not ripe. When it is, Miss Elliott, you'll be the first to know.'

For some reason Victoria felt embarrassed. 'Yes, well, I'm sorry if I spoke out of turn. Do you think Dr Mackie will be ready for us by now?'

'Yes,' Dugald assented quietly. 'Yes, I'm sure he will be. Let's go.'

He bent to Hairylegs, who was still worshipping the benign Number Seven, and clipped on his lead.

# CHAPTER EIGHT

DR MACKIE, courteous and, despite the hour, quite unperturbed, did not keep them long. The episode could have been another proof of the respect in which Dugald was held. Victoria was given the necessary injection and Dugald took her home.

As they neared the head of the glen he slowed up and stopped. 'Shall we walk the rest of the way? It would be a pity to wake Lorraine.'

The good intentions, however, were vain. Lorraine was at the window. She flung the hall door open and came down the path to meet them.

'What's happened? Where have you been? I've been out of my mind.'

The miscreant white terrier had arrived back an hour ago and his howls at the door had alerted her to the situation.

'I'm sorry,' Victoria began. 'I didn't think ...'

'Then you should have.' The sharpness was proof that Lorraine was overwrought.

'I didn't think you'd miss me,' Victoria continued patiently. 'I looked in, and you were asleep. I decided not to wake you.'

'You're too fond of taking chances. I never know what you'll do.'

'Lorraine.' Dugald's voice stemmed the flow of words. 'I'd like to talk to you. May I have five minutes?'

'Yes. Is it bad news?' Lorraine was coming back to herself. She was now only concerned. 'You *are* all right, Vic?'

'Of course. Look at me.' Victoria too was slipping into her customary role of protector. 'And look at you,

you chump. Put something warm on. You'll freeze.'

Lorraine's wrap and nightie, both from her trousseau, were real Hollywood stuff, filmy white with a lot of lace and ribbon. Her hair floated on her shoulders. Now that anger had evaporated Victoria could have kicked herself. She had acted impulsively, made the wrong decision. Lorraine obviously had been worried—stiff.

'I'll make you a hot drink,' she said quickly.

'No, *I* will. I want to talk to her,' Dugald interposed 'And I want *you* to go to bed. Doctor's orders, so far as I remember.'

It was another battle of wills, but the strain of the past few hours, possibly coupled with Dr Mackie's injection, was threatening to blot her out. The last thing she could have stood now was an altercation. 'Goodnight, then. You win.'

Dugald looked at her sternly. 'Not often enough.' His face softened. 'Goodnight, soldier. Sleep well.'

It was a command Victoria's tired body could not disobey. She woke refreshed to a sunny morning and thought of the day ahead—the nut and bolt man would be coming, it was clinic night, and in between she needed to buy stores. One things was certain—it was a case of 'get up and go'.

She ran a bath and pulled off her nightdress. It was a pink shift patterned with tiny coloured apples. Victoria liked fun and had wintered cosily in sweeping red flannel. But it was suddenly a speaking contrast to lace and white nylon.

'And that,' Victoria told herself, 'is an odd thought to have, very odd indeed.'

Just the same it lingered, pinpointing aspects which at the time she had been too exhausted to see in depth— not only Lorraine's quickness to calm down and abandon her anger but Dugald's look of tenderness and the arm he had laid so naturally on her shoulders.

Bathed and dry, Victoria put on a short housecoat of brown towelling and went downstairs.

Lorraine was already up, breakfast was on the table and Sandy Gibson, true to Dugald's promise, was examining the bolts on the hutches.

'Don't go out like that!' Lorraine called sharply as Victoria opened the door into the garden. 'You're not dressed.'

'I'm not going to let this one get away,' Victoria retorted.

It was a satisfactory if costly interview. Sandy Gibson, undoubtedly spurred by Dugald's interest, made many useful suggestions on security and promised to go into Selkirk that morning for the necessary materials. He would start the job some time during the afternoon.

'Thank goodness for that,' Victoria reported jubilantly as she arrived back at the breakfast table. Another hurdle had been crossed. A heavier outlay than anticipated, but she felt sure the workmanship would be good. 'In for a penny, in for a pound.'

Lorraine had been listening a shade too quietly. 'Vic, I wish you wouldn't spend all that money.'

'It is a lot, I agree.' Victoria munched happily. 'But we must give it the right name. It's an investment in the future.'

'That's just it.' Lorraine fidgeted. 'I don't think we should stay for ever.'

'Who said anything about "for ever"?' Comprehension began to dawn. Victoria looked searchingly at her sister's face. 'Lorrie, what is this? You want to pack it in *now*?'

'Not want to—feel it would be wise. Dugald and I had a long talk last night. I don't know if you realise how anxious he is about you.'

'I realise how anxious he is to get his hands on this place.'

'Now stop, Vic, that's not fair.' Lorraine had flushed.
'He's been a good friend. Look how he's helped us out.'

That was the nub of it. Victoria's anger trickled
away in sad cold drops. He had helped, he had been
kind and practical and at times uncannily perceptive.
And last night on the hill she had allowed herself to
think that they were friends.

For days now she had been content to leave it that
Mr Bradley, the owner of the expensive holiday cottage,
had been the complainant. *Content.* She hurled the
word relentlessly in her own teeth. It was more than
that. 'You don't want it to be Dugald,' she accused herself. 'Why?'

'I gather you talked me over,' she said tightly.

'Yes, but don't look at it that way,' Lorraine begged.
'We knew you were too tired to join in. Vic, I think
you should sell to Dugald. He'll give you five per cent
more than the valuation, and he'll talk to the animal
people, he has friends on their council and he's sure
they'll find room for Charlie and any others in their
new home and rest centre near Galashiels. It's not offi-
cially open yet and they've got an enormous debt on it,
that's why he thought you might like the extra five per
cent...'

'I wouldn't like it at all.' Victoria paused to regain
control of her emotions. 'It's not on, Lorrie. No way.
But it doesn't involve you. I want you to know that.
Wild Heart wasn't left jointly, it's mine. You are as free
as air.' Somehow she couldn't bear to continue. 'We'll
talk about it again. I should go and see what's to be
done with those strays Ellen mentioned.'

A cat had been rearing her family in a ruined cottage
the far side of the village. Ellen had seen boys torment-
ing them and was in any case anxious to see them
housed before the weather turned cold. Victoria had
not planned to tackle the problem for a day or so, but

suddenly it was all-important to get away.

She took two baskets, baited them with fish and sat down hopefully to wait.

It was a long time since she had felt so miserable. Last night had been hectic, arduous, even dangerous. Terrified as she had felt at times, it had been preferable to this low-key depression.

There was nothing new in Lorraine's arguments. What hurt was that they had discussed her behind her back. Dugald had made tea and then Lorrie and he had talked for almost an hour.

Nothing, of course, could be done without her agreement, and indeed Lorraine had run out to the car as she was leaving to say warmly: 'I won't leave you in the lurch, Vic. It's not that. I like the place.'

So what was it? The possibility she had discounted a week ago, that Dugald might like Lorraine as much as she obviously liked him, that their relationship might have a future, that in fact the best solution imaginable for Lorraine, the cure that had seemed too much to hope for, might have come about?

'Victoria Elliott,' she concluded roundly, 'you don't know a miracle when you see it, thank your stars for this one.'

It was a hot afternoon. She put the new acquisitions into a separate pen till she could have them vetted. They looked healthy and were surprisingly tame, so she judged the mother had been a pet and was used to being handled. It improved their chances of finding permanent homes.

The handyman had not returned from his shopping spree and Lorraine volunteered to wait for him while Victoria went to buy the stores they needed.

'If you're going to be here we can let the chickens out,' Victoria decreed, and did so.

She had purposely not returned to the subject of the

115

sale, but she felt that Lorraine was thinking of it when she said affectionately: 'You really love this place, don't you?'

'That I do,' Victoria mused as, some time later, she drove back to it with a laden car. She longed to see every season in the glen, to experience its storms and its frosty calms and to share its snow at Christmas. She pictured the short afternoons with lights going on in the windows and she thought about Tango with his ruff grown.

She could relate to the force that drove Dugald to work so hard. He was no longer rich, but his roots were in Baldougrie and he would never let it go. She hoped Lorraine realised that Dugald's wife must also be his helpmeet. Gutsy. Not afraid of hard work. Wearing tough clothes. Ready to try her hand at anything.

Except that, if gossip was correct, the love to whom he had remained so faithful had not been a bit like that. He had been graced by her presence, it had been all the reward he asked.

As she took the fork to the elbow and the brown roof of Wild Heart came into view, she heard a scream. More came to her as she accelerated. The voice was girlish, panic-stricken and familiar. Lorraine's.

Victoria stopped the car and tumbled out. She was conscious that a running figure had beaten her to the gate and dashed round the corner into the garden.

'Oh, cripes, the fox!' Magnus's voice rang out. He gave a long whistle. 'He's done it this time, hasn't he?'

Victoria, hard on his heels, found a scene of mayhem. The intruder seemed to have killed in all directions. It was horrible, ghastly; she couldn't bear to look. Three were left alive and Magnus hustled them into the hen-house.

While Victoria tried to soothe Lorraine, he picked up a dead chicken.

'How many did you have?' There was something reminiscent about his reaction. He was only a child, but he had stayed calm.

It was more than poor Lorraine had done. She was still hysterical.

'We had ten,' Victoria answered.

Magnus counted out five dead fowl. It left two missing.

'Better look for them,' he said pertinently. 'If you don't want them falling into the wrong hands—or should I say the wrong teeth?'

Victoria was sickened by the carnage. She prided herself on not turning her back on unpleasantness, but this was too much. She took Lorraine still shuddering into the house and put her into a chair.

'Cup of tea coming right up,' she said more cheerfully than she felt.

It had been a wretched experience. Lorraine had gone out to sunbathe on the strip of lawn and nodded off. By the time the chickens' frenzied clucking had roused her, it had been too late. The fox had been amongst them. She had seen the flash of his brush.

'Oh, Vic, I'll never forget it!'

'You *will*,' Victoria comforted. 'Drink that tea and stop blaming yourself. It wasn't *you* let them out.'

It was time to go and help Magnus, who had assumed responsibility in such a peculiar way. After all, they did not even know his surname.

She went out and there he was, unsentimentally gathering up the dead.

'You can cook them,' he explained.

Sandy Gibson had just arrived; half an hour earlier and his presence might have averted the tragedy. Victoria left him to get on with the job and went with Magnus to find the two missing chickens. It was pathetic to picture the effort these had made to save their

117

heads. One was discovered hiding under a thorn bush halfway up the side of the glen.

Magnus lifted it, clucking and fluttering, into his arms. Yuk, Victoria thought ashamedly, could I have done that?

'I'll take it back. You go on looking,' he commanded. 'Don't get lost.'

Victoria had not lost sight of the disaster aspect, but it was fast being overshadowed by curiosity. Who was Magnus? Invariably he seemed to appear from nowhere, invariably he brought a message for the particular situation.

She continued the search as instructed even in unlikely places. The thickets were rich in harts' tongue fern and carpeted with ivy and the orangey red berries of woody nightshade. There were pale dead branches like clutching fingers but, alas, no brown hen.

The thicket thinned and she found herself back on an open part of the brae. Simultaneously she saw below her a dot of brown moving across the green. Forgetting how hard she might find it to stop, Victoria set off down the slope at a gallop. She gathered impetus as she ran, her toes catching in the tussocks of grass, and then, not surprisingly, she lost her footing and fell, rolling over a couple of times before she felt herself being picked up.

'Proving, I take it, that the rolling stone gathers no moss?' It was Craig who had come to the rescue. He set her on her feet and stood holding her for several minutes longer than necessary.

'Oh lor'!' Victoria rubbed her elbow. 'I didn't see you.'

Craig was not the fussing kind. He said gaily: 'Talk about pennies from heaven!'

In the middle of the pleasantries a new voice cut in: 'Are you all right, Victoria? You could have hurt yourself.' Dugald with a pup on a choke collar was standing some yards away. She realised to her chagrin that he had been with Craig at the time of her tumble.

'I didn't.' Pride made the lie excusable. And pride was smarting more than her grazed elbow.

As an attempt to end the matter, it failed. 'Please don't try that again,' Dugald warned. 'You could break a leg. There are rabbit holes all over the brae.'

Must she always be made to look a fool? It was vexatious in the extreme. Equally disappointing was the fact that Craig, disliking differences as much as she did herself, was about to make his getaway.

'See you at the clinic!' he called cheerfully. 'Don't be late.'

She couldn't blame him, but she wished he had stayed. One was always at ease with Craig. He had a step as light as his tongue, she thought, as she watched him go.

Dugald was watching too. When she turned round his gaze was resting on her as though he realised the comparison she was making.

'I take it you weren't risking your limbs without reason. What seems to be the trouble?'

She made it brief and casual, partly for Lorraine's sake, partly for her own. A lecture seemed inevitable, but surprisingly she heard a sound of sympathy.

'That's too bad. Now I understand the hurry. Where did you see the hen?'

Almost before she could point to the place, he had spotted and retrieved the runaway. It squawked as he bore it back. It was Hobson's choice, carry it or put up with Dugald's company. Victoria made a bold decision —the chicken. She went to take it and found herself ignored.

To expect him to understand her feelings was futile, but her monosyllabic replies must have communicated some of them. 'Have I offended you?' Dugald asked abruptly.

'Since you ask, yes. I have always found it offensive to have my future disposed of without a by-your-leave.'

'I presume you're referring to my conversation with Lorraine?'

'At least you don't deny it.'

'I regret it,' he said quietly. 'It was an error of judgment and it should never have been relayed to you. That was unfortunate. My apologies.' As Victoria stared he went on smoothly: 'I hope you will have dinner with me some night in the near future to allow me to ventilate the matter at first hand.'

Victoria could not understand why she should suddenly want to laugh.

'Oh well, that's rather a drastic recompense,' she deprecated.

'You seem to inspire me to drastic measures. Do you accept?'

She was astonished to find herself blushing. 'If I'm free!'

'Then at least permit me to take my place in the queue,' he requested gravely.

As they traversed the last fifty yards to Wild Heart, Victoria took the opportunity of asking if he knew Magnus, who seemed once again to have done his disappearing trick. She had had a queer notion that he had been watching them, perhaps from behind a tree, but though she had glanced back once or twice he had not broken cover.

'You think there's some mystery about him?' Dugald looked amused.

'I think he hides himself,' Victoria said thoughtfully. 'And to me he seems out of place. I don't know why exactly, except that he's always alone and never mentions a family. I keep getting the impression that he's a lonely child, again I don't know why.'

'And——' The prompt was sharp, almost uneasy.

'I just thought that if you knew him there might be something I could do. In return for the help he's given us.'

'That's kind of you.' Dugald paused. 'Magnus probably needs companionship and seems to have found it. In that case, the thanks are equal.'

Apparently he had drawn a blank. He did not know Magnus and, as anticipated, there was no sign of the boy at Wild Heart.

Sandy Gibson made a good job of the fencing and other fastenings; Dugald's presence undoubtedly helped. He stayed to oversee after he had brought back the hen. The five surviving chickens were safely under cover and there seemed a lot more room. It gave Victoria a strange feeling of sadness.

'I'm sorry,' she said suddenly. 'I never thought I would be, but I am.'

Oddly, it seemed to go further than that. The hens had been a bone of contention from the start, Dugald seeming to have a special interest in them. She thought he must be angry and regretful to see it come to this.

'You liked them, didn't you?' she faltered. 'I'm sorry.'

For a moment she thought he was going to laugh. Then his gaze softened. 'My dear girl, I believe you really mean it!'

He had touched a spring. Victoria felt compassion siphoning to the surface, not for the minor tragedy of the chickens but for the other man-size loss and the gap that still remained.

She felt like crying out: 'Lorrie loves you and she's good. Be happy, my dear. You won't be breaking faith.'

But she stayed silent, the fountain of words frozen and her heart thundering through her chest.

It was a pain that turned the world upside down, old

and incurable, a pain that made gods weep. And it was wild, wild as the wind and the odds that had brought her to the glen.

In short, it was love.

'Don't fret about the chickens,' Dugald was saying kindly. 'It's true I once thought they were your only asset. But not now.' He clasped her arm briefly and paternally. 'You're a brave bonny lass and you do *my* side no good.'

Dugald had spent so much time with Sandy Gibson that Lorraine pressed him to stay for supper and for once he accepted. It would be a nice meal; Lorraine was an excellent cook, and it had the advantage of taking her mind off her unpleasant experience. Victoria could not join the party. Craig had warned her not to be late for the clinic, and as well she had promised to collect an old age pensioner and her dog.

'Pity the poor workers,' she said lightly, preparing to leave.

'Oh, Vic, do stay. It's your favourite,' Lorraine protested.

It was a relief that she could not accede. After the shock of her feeling for Dugald Victoria's one thought was to get away.

A drizzle of rain was falling as she reached the surgery and the small group of clients waiting for the door to be opened looked disgruntled. One bolder than the rest called out: 'Ask him will he no' let us in. We're fair soaked!'

'Well, a rule is a rule,' Victoria deprecated. 'And you are a little early. Perhaps some of you could sit in the car.' She opened the doors invitingly. 'If so, you're very welcome.'

'Your aunt was always speakin' to him about lettin' us in,' she was assured. 'Och, I don't know where we'll be without her.'

Victoria, slipping round to Craig's entrance, felt embarrassed and additionally depressed. He noticed this at once.

'That's right,' he said, beaming, when she repeated the conversation about Aunt Elizabeth. 'She did speak to me. If I'd a bawbee for the number of times she rapped my knuckles I'd be a wealthy man. So what, my darling? The tail can't wag the dog. It also so happens that they don't pay. All in all, I don't think they've much to moan about.

'And they'll have to wait a bit longer,' he added, unabashed. 'Something urgent has come up.'

An emergency? Victoria speculated, wondering if she could stand up to the sight of blood. It turned out to be a blown fuse. Craig set about tracing it and called down to her cheerily from the top of a ladder.

'You've got a date for Saturday, by the way. I'm doing my thing at a Champion Show the far side of Galashiels. The pickings will be good, so come and share them. You'll enjoy it.

'I won't take no for an answer,' he concluded, withdrawing his head from the fuse cupboard.

'I wasn't going to say no,' Victoria retorted. He was a rogue, but he would keep her from brooding. The invitation was a godsend.

# CHAPTER NINE

DUGALD had mentioned the show some weeks ago and by a coincidence only that evening had renewed his suggestion that they should attend it with him. Lorraine passed on the invitation at breakfast next morning and seemed disappointed that Victoria had already accepted Craig's.

'No harm done,' Victoria said briskly. 'We're sure to bump into each other.'

That she should be in love with Dugald was hysterical, a mirage. Something to do with the heather and the faded kilt. But love was not new to her. She always knew what she was doing. As now.

He was attractive and she had reacted. Would she have been a woman if she had not? The important thing was not to fool herself that it could ever be anything more.

Lorraine was still talking. Dugald had an entry in the puppy class and was also giving the Number Seven a shot at his championship. On points he should have no difficulty in winning his third and quota certificate, but there was a question mark over how he would show.

'Aunt Elizabeth has a lot to answer for,' she concluded virtuously.

'Don't forget, so has Dugald,' Victoria corrected.

'I thought we'd decided the complaint about the hutches came from Mr Bradley.'

'How can we without proof?' Victoria pushed back her chair. A romantic might have convinced herself that Dugald was guiltless; Victoria couldn't. She had too searching a mind.

She went outside and discovered Magnus in a royal

blue anorak. He pointed to a bird that was hovering overhead and told her it was a kestrel. 'At least I think so. What do you say?'

Victoria had no opinion to offer and clearly he was disappointed. It seemed crucial that his identification should be confirmed. A complex child, but one whose aloofness drew her.

'What happened to you yesterday?' she tackled. 'I thought you were coming back to find that hen.'

'Oh yes. It wasn't convenient.'

'Mr Douglas wouldn't have eaten you.' She made a final attempt.

'I daresay.' Magnus continued to stare at the kestrel. Without looking at her he made her a proposition—himself, as part-time kennel-man. He could promise no more than two hours daily, but she was sure he could satisfy her on performance. It was a careful offer and the phrasing would have done credit to someone twice his age. She felt certain it was also a plea for company.

'You're on. Starting from now. Just one thing we haven't mentioned—when do you go back to school?'

'Oh, that.' He seemed to think for a minute. 'Can we say I'll let you know? My movements are a bit uncertain.'

She had got a bargain. Food was allocated, dogs exercised, grasses cut and errands run all with the minimum of wordage. 'Mastermind', as she called him privately, was no blabbermouth.

'I can't think what we did without him,' Victoria remarked on Saturday. That week for the first time since coming to Strathfin she had been able to get down to some writing and Lorraine had had time to make a batch of biscuits. 'How nice that looks on you,' she added warmly as her sister came into the bedroom ready for the day's outing.

The cotton dress was one Victoria herself had

brought from America as a contribution to the wedding trousseau. It was red with a flounced hemline and appliqué panels. It was also the latest lower calf length. Lorrie had greeted it with a startled look and Victoria had wondered if she would ever wear it. But on the new Lorraine, it, like the trousers, was a clear success.

Craig had intimated an early start, so Victoria had to speed up her own toilet. A practised hand applied soft grey eye-shadow and a pinky brown lipstick, and brushed round her bouncy hair. She had both designed and made her dirndl skirt and quilted waistcoat. They were border printed cotton and went over a deep pink shirt. Her sole accessory was a wide pink bangle. The whole was a fresh peasanty look and it suited her.

'You look like the icing on the cake,' Craig said cheerily. 'When do I get my first bite?'

He drove fast using the main roads. Now and again it occurred to Victoria that beneath the banter lived a highly organised person. Small blame to him for that, she conceded, as she watched the vetting process.

The show scene was new to her. Judging had not yet begun, but it was fascinating to see the last-minute preparations on the benches. A Maltese terrier wearing a bow on its topknot. A final flick up to a poodle's curls. A St Bernard standing as high as the tot who was grooming it.

Disconcertingly, Craig did not seem all that interested in events. As soon as he was free they joined up with a party of his friends, including Jim Redfern from the *Argus*, and headed towards the bar and refreshment marquee. The excellent cold buffet was on the house for officials and their guests.

'We mustn't miss the Labradors.' Victoria had the Number Seven on her mind.

Craig looked amused. 'Sounds like a good title for a book.' There was plenty of time, he added, and her plate

126

was empty. That wouldn't do. 'More salmon?'

When she shook her head, Jim Redfern jumped up and procured a dish of mixed fruit and a jug of cream.

'Hands off,' Craig warned gaily. 'This is my woman. I saw her first.'

Victoria was tickled. 'You flatter me, gentlemen, but the one that saw me first has four legs and, please, I must see if he's going to end up a champ.'

'What's she on about?' one of the girls in the party demanded.

'It's a bee she gets in her bonnet at times.' Was it imagination that Craig's smile was a little forced? 'It's in the blood, you know. She's Elizabeth Elliott's niece.'

'Well, I'm blowed!' A man in the group lowered his glass to stare, appraisingly. Only a fool could fail to read his thoughts. 'It doesn't show,' he said kindly.

Victoria had to ask her way to the ring where the gundogs were being shown. It had been subdivided for the various breeds, setters, spaniels, pointers and, in the farthest corner, the Labrador retrievers. She hurried across noting the light elegance of an Irish setter and smiled at the despair of a child whose cocker spaniel refused to stand up.

A lady in the gallery of spectators shook her head when Victoria asked anxiously if the Labradors had been judged. 'But you're only just in time. Here she comes now to judge the puppies.'

Victoria's eyes skimmed the crowd for a flash of tartan, but Dugald didn't seem to be there, and disappointment turned into disgust at herself. How Aunt Elizabeth would despise this interest in an enemy!

She had noticed a young man with a microphone a few yards away from her and as the puppies and their handlers got ready he opened up. The spectator, who had answered Victoria's question about the judging, glanced at him and smiled: 'Listen to him. He's quite good fun. I think he's doing a feature for the local station.'

The commentator was giving a brief rundown on the history of the Labrador and its distinctive characteristics. 'It's a matter of personal taste,' he concluded. 'But I like them to have brown eyes.'

'The rascal! He's looking at you!' Victoria's companion whispered.

Behind them the commentator continued: 'And there they go, the champions of tomorrow—all looking good, a nice circle, walking with their handlers. And there's a nice piece of window-dressing, one that I'm sure would make Walter Douglas very proud if he were here to see it. The puppy from Baldougrie is being handled by the new member of the firm, Magnus McAlester, and like his grandfather before him, he's wearing a kilt. A kilt, of course, in his own tartan. Well, we're a hospitable lot here in the Borders. There'll be no fighting among the clans today.'

Hearers in the vicinity chuckled. Victoria's friend pointed, but it was unnecessary. Long before the commentator had spoken, Victoria's eyes had fastened incredulously on the familiar flaxen head. Impossible! No, it was so obvious that she should have rumbled it from the first. The invisible 'M. McAlester' and the mysterious Magnus were one and the same: Dugald's nephew. As solitary and friendless as he seemed? Or a plant? Another subtle way of putting Wild Heart under an obligation to Baldougrie?

If the latter, it meant she had won no battle. Magnus had made his offer out of obedience rather than liking.

She stared at the black pup, now giving a mischievous tug to its master's red kilt.

The circle stopped moving and the judge called the first pair and began the usual detailed examination of the dog. It would not be Magnus's turn for some minutes. Magnus—as always her heart went out to him. The shoulder-tabbed jacket gave him breadth, but he was so still, so serious. Have I ever seen him laugh? Victoria asked herself.

'That was a nice reference to Walter Douglas,' her companion suddenly observed. 'He was a founder of this show. You never met him, I suppose?' When Victoria shook her head she went on to talk about Dugald's father, painting a vivid picture in the way one does when one is very fond of the subject. Walter Douglas had been a big man, standing head and shoulders over everyone else in a room. His character had been written in his face. He had had bright dark eyes, fiery when roused but mostly full of fun. And he would give you the shirt off his back. He had pioneered dog training in the area and had bred such beautiful Labradors that the Baldougrie strain was known by breeders the world over. 'We felt so sad when he died,' the speaker concluded. 'Because his son had his own career and we didn't really expect he would carry on.'

She stopped as the judge came to Magnus and the pup 'Black Gold'. To Victoria the set-up looked excellent. The puppy was docile and stood as though on a plinth. Magnus had placed it laboriously. He walked it forward and back with the same measured care. Somewhat disappointingly, Victoria's companion, though she watched intently, had nothing to say.

Victoria thought fearfully about the Number Seven. He could so easily rebel against the discipline.

'My sister and I know Dugald Douglas in a business way.' Suddenly she was unable to keep her fears to herself. 'I wish I could be as sure of his other dog—I mean, from the behaviour angle.' Her companion looked inquiring. 'Today could make him a champion, but he's quite likely to stand up and put his arms round the judge's neck or bolt through her legs and knock her

129

over. And if he does, my great-aunt will be to blame. She had him for a while and—his training got neglected.'

'Had him?'

'Quite truthfully, she kidnapped him,' Victoria confessed. 'I think the term is "enticement". Dugald saw how fond they were of each other and seems to have let things ride. Then she died and Number Seven went back to Baldougrie. Dugald has been giving him the most intensive training ever since, but my sister says he's not really sure of him yet.'

She thought her companion's attention had wandered to the next stage of the puppy competition as the bitches came up for judging. A black one, her tongue sideways in a casual grin, earned a spurt of applause. Victoria's new acquaintance did not join in, but she looked approving.

It was exciting to notice that Magnus and Black Gold had been pulled out of the Dog section. Victoria's eyes were glued to the ring. She almost resented the interruption when her companion said abruptly: 'I don't think I caught your name.'

'Victoria Elliott. My great-aunt had a small animal refuge in Strathfin. She left it to me.'

'I knew her well and liked her. She was a most interesting person.' The eyes meeting Victoria's seemed suddenly extra intelligent, as though they knew and were saying a lot more than the words.

'She was a darling,' Victoria said shakily. 'And I should have come years ago. That's the trouble. The years made her less law-abiding, that's all. And her love carried her away. There was trouble.' The other nodded. 'But in the matter of the dog Dugald was forbearing.'

'Dugald is like his father.' It was quietly said. 'A greatheart.'

The words seemed to echo as the judge extended her arm and pointed to the happy-looking black bitch. In the same second Victoria found herself alone. Her companion had glanced at her watch, smiled and hastened away. A moment later, to her intense disappointment, Victoria heard the commentator confirm that Best of Breed had not been given to the Baldougrie puppy.

'Well, bad luck there for young Magnus McAlester and Black Gold. The judge gave it to the bitch, but a nice piece of handling for a first attempt. Nothing his grandfather would have been ashamed of. I prophesy we shall see a lot more of this pair.'

Victoria had not realised that Craig and the others were near her in the crowd. 'We saw *you*,' Craig said pointedly. She wondered at the searching look, but next instant it went out of her head. His plans for the evening were a sixsome with Jim and three others, objective a party, eighty-eight miles away in Dundee.

Victoria blinked, but for every demur he had an answer. Easy hostess, open house, the more casual the dress the better. As to the time of homecoming— 'Well, honestly, my darling, I've not got that far. There are always beds, you know—in Dundee.'

'This has been a beautiful day, Craig,' Victoria said steadily. 'Shall we say enough is as good as a feast?'

'What you mean is you're fed up. You didn't like Tom making that crack about your great-aunt and you're taking it out on me.'

'I hope I'm more discriminating than that. But it was an unfunny joke. Or don't you think so?'

'Of course I think so. If you hadn't slipped away so fast you'd have heard me choke him off. So does that equalise? And I should think before you drop your friendly vet in the wrong hands.'

'You're a fool!' Victoria tried not to see the wheedling smile.

'Many a true word spoken in jest. So what about it, duckie? Yes or no?'

She supposed it was fate that supplied the perfect timing. Craig was a difficult person to refuse; he was a good friend, a friend she needed, and plainly he wanted her company. But Victoria did not want to go to Dundee and she was relieved beyond measure to see Dugald and Lorraine approaching.

Lorraine's cheeks were pink. She had about her a gentle air of happiness. Dugald had a hand on her arm. He was wearing a blue herringbone jacket dull enough to avoid a clash with the Douglas tartan. Obviously he was hurrying to the show ring, but he stopped to ask Victoria if she was enjoying herself.

It was a kind little gesture, one which if you skipped back in time she was sure his father would have made. 'A greatheart', that nice anonymous woman had said.

And then she heard Craig explaining about the party in Dundee.

'I haven't said I was going,' she put in.

'But speaking as your astrologer I say you will.'

It was becoming a tedious wrangle, but she had no intention of yielding. None, that is, until Dugald suddenly rapped out: 'Dundee? A party tonight? With you and Redfern?'

'And others. Why?' Craig still sounded amused.

'I forbid it,' Dugald said brusquely. 'Victoria will come home with us.'

Even Lorraine looked taken aback. Craig's golden forehead developed frown lines of puzzlement. Victoria quite simply had neither words nor breath.

Dugald was 'forbidding' her? That was what he had said, and by his steely face that was he had meant. But people did not 'forbid' unless they had a right or a responsibility.

'Did you say "forbid"?' she echoed. It was almost funny, and a laugh crept into her voice.

'Does that seem so extraordinary?' he challenged. 'You've had a day out with the usual embellishments. You're proposing to drive eighty-eight miles to a party, inevitably drink some more and then face the return journey. The extraordinary thing to me is that you should consider it in the first place.'

'Would you mind repeating that I've had too much to drink?' Victoria requested softly.

'Don't twist my words. I never said that. You're sober. So is he.' The implacable eyes rested for a second on Craig. 'Others in your party are not.'

'I'm not going with the others.'

'You're not going at all,' Dugald returned.

'Upon my soul,' Victoria said vexedly, 'you force me...'

'That's right.' Unexpectedly he put his hand out and drew her a few paces away. 'If we're quibbling about a word, will "favour" suit you better?'

Victoria blinked.

'As a favour to me, will you come home sanely and sensibly with us?' He was enough of a tactician to ride trivialities. Words, for instance, could be discarded like spent bullets.

'Stick to handling the Number Seven,' she advised. 'He's more credulous than I am and there's more at stake.'

'You could be putting your *life* at stake,' Dugald said quietly. 'Should that not matter to a friend?'

Victoria told herself that it was not giving in. There were many reasons apart from Dugald Douglas why she should not go to Dundee. But it was Dugald's eyes, bluer for the new kilt jacket, that made her blush, and she could not deny the fact.

'All right, I'll go along with that,' she said shortly.

Craig took it well; she could only hope that the joking: 'Well, nice to have known you!' did not conceal deep hurt.

Dugald had gone to pick up the Number Seven, so she had an opportunity of pumping Lorraine on the subject of Magnus. But Lorraine could not be of much help. She had been astonished to see him in the car when Dugald had called for her and all she had gathered was that his parents were abroad.

Meantime the atmosphere was hotting up. The exhibitors were assembling and she could see Dugald and the Number Seven. The dog was laughing quietly to himself. Given half a chance and he would plunge through his repertoire, fawning, giving the paw, forging ahead.

'That's just what I told ...' Victoria did not finish the sentence. Her eyes widened disbelievingly as the judge walked into the ring. 'Lordy! I've just been talking to her. I didn't know who she was.'

'Did you say anything you shouldn't?' Lorraine asked pertinently.

Victoria didn't think so. In fact on reflection it seemed a good thing, because the Number Seven had his own show style and, as anticipated, it was not in the least statuesque. But better than that, it won him Best of Breed.

So much was bound up in that dog, reward for effort, justification of the second chance, vindication for an old lady whose spoiling had after all done no lasting damage. Victoria was too jubilant to stand still. She grabbed Lorraine and hugged her in silent ecstasy.

It was only the beginning.

There followed the judging of gundog against gundog. Incredibly, it went to a cliffhanger between the Number Seven and an Irish setter bitch.

'These two dogs are quite different,' the commentator

announced. 'The bitch is concentrating hard. The Labrador is a "Laughing Cavalier". His handler in fact is using only fingertip control. A very experienced handler, this, and very popular, Dugald Douglas from Baldougrie.'

Victoria was a novice. She watched the judge uncertainly.

'And it's the Labrador,' the young man behind her had no doubt at all. 'The Labrador's got it. The setter is reserve. The Labrador wins the group.'

There was hardly time to grasp the miracle and none at all for congratulations; the gundogs were the last to be creamed off and the show was running late. Within minutes the final six were lining up, a Cairn terrier, a Dalmatian, a German Shepherd, a King Charles spaniel, an Afghan hound, and the Number Seven. The Afghan was a nice red dog with a black mask. The Dalmatian was strong-boned with big round spots. Victoria wavered between them and settled for the Afghan.

'He's the one,' she said pessimistically. He was showy and exotic. They wouldn't pass him by.

'I think he looks cadaverous,' Lorraine objected loyally.

Victoria turned away from the Number Seven, who was looking puzzled but benign, because quite simply she couldn't bear it. He wouldn't win—for no other reason than that she wanted it so abnormally. It was a private silliness; she had always tried to fool the gods by pretending not to care.

This time it wasn't going to work. The judge had touched the Afghan and a storm of clapping had broken out. The shock of it made Victoria go hot, then disappointment hollowed her and she felt sick.

And then she saw that the Afghan was being led away —and in fact all the dogs except the Number Seven.

At the same time, to clinch it, came the commentator's voice: 'And this great happy dog—a dog which, if you'll pardon the whimsy, reminds me a bit of Walter Douglas himself—has come right through effortlessly to take the premier award here today. Best in Show, 1976, Mr Dugald Douglas's Baldougrie Number Seven!'.

The crowd made it difficult to get to the meeting place with Dugald and to her astonishment Victoria was waylaid by two fashion-conscious teenagers who had overheard her name. They were likeable youngsters, but they took time. When they had gone Lorraine reported that she had seen someone come up and say something to Dugald. 'That newspaper man, I think, Jim Redfern. I can't see either of them now.'

When they reached him, Magnus was packing up. Bench chains, rugs, water bowls and grooming kit went item by item into a holdall. Lorraine went to assist, Victoria gravitated naturally to her first love.

'Oh, Number Seven, I am so proud of you,' she said tremulously. The dog, pressing his mild face into her skirt, could not know how much of the past he had salvaged.

When she looked up, Dugald had come back and was watching them. For how long? she wondered embarrassedly, as she jumped up to give her congratulations. He acknowledged them with a smile. 'If that means what it looked like Seven is a fortunate dog.'

'I thought that wretched Afghan had beaten him, and I couldn't have borne it.' Not strictly true, but a forgivable extravagance.

Dugald continued to look at her with that twist of smile. It stirred a vague memory which for the moment she let go.

'I've had an idea,' he said. 'We're so near Abbotsford,

it seems a pity not to pay it a visit. It will still be open if we move fast.'

Undoubtedly a kindness, but unnecessary. Victoria had no wish to disrupt the proceedings. Abbotsford, home of Sir Walter Scott, was a must, but it could wait. She started to say so and was interrupted: 'Right, then. We're all here. Let's go.' One hand took hold of Seven's leash, the other grasped Black Gold's. And somehow you didn't argue with Dugald in this mood. He led off across the car park and Victoria followed with Magnus and Lorraine.

It was in her mind that Dugald, breasting his way between the two dogs, must resemble his ancestors who had kept the Scottish Marches. No one could quite escape their past, and Dugald's had gone to make up a very special man. Brown rugged face, wide back, hands as well kept as a doctor's. Beautiful old tartan. Native tweed. Shoes to which polishing had brought a bloom.

It was the kind of look Victoria herself went for. Shining hair and very clean denims, a glowing skin.

Hers was a hopeless love, but it had its comforts. That thought of likeness was one of them.

If she had been less preoccupied she would, at that stage, have sensed that something was happening. The public address system crackled, recalling certain exhibitors to the ring, and already a sort of whisper, excited and incredulous, was running through the crowd. It was the way news travelled and all her life she had been attuned to it. But keeping up with Dugald, she did not look back.

Five minutes at the most and they were under way.

Abbotsford was balm for the most wistful heart. There was first the sight of its turrets in the trees across the Tweed and then the spit of intense green, like an arrowhead, where the river met the Ettrick Water. There were fields where wild flowers had taken over, a yellow carpet of hawkbit, a blood-red scarf of poppies. And at last the courts and cloister screen of Abbotsford House with the stone effigy of Maida, Sir Walter's deerhound, by the entrance porch.

Dugald gave Magnus the admission tickets and said he would follow when the dogs had stretched their legs. 'Enjoy yourselves. Don't rush. There's a lot to see.' He stopped to buy a guide book which he handed to Lorraine.

Watching, it struck Victoria that here lay the explanation for their dash from the show ground. Lorraine, she was sure, had had an enjoyable day, but when it came to comparison she would find Abbotsford much more to her taste. It was just one more instance of Dugald's liking and consideration for her. He had displayed both from the moment they met.

As with Lorraine. She had made no attempt to disguise her feelings. And she had blossomed. From being a lovely shadow she had changed to a real person, and a very dear one. Victoria could not grudge her this happiness and she didn't. It complicated the future, but that was nobody's problem but her own.

The world knew the story of Sir Walter Scott, his love for the Tweed valley, the house which enshrined his interest in the age of chivalry, and how he had turned himself into a writing machine to clear the debts his partners had incurred. His presence seemed to cling to the walls of Abbotsford. His chair was still drawn to the desk in his study, the spiral staircase from his bedroom still testified to his practice of going down to write in the small hours, and the lovely white and hazel brown dining-room—the room in which he had died— still gave the same loved view of the river.

Victoria pictured a tired man resting his eyes on the scene, his pen laid down but his heroes riding before him along the banks of the Tweed—Marmion, Rob Roy, Ivanhoe, Lochinvar.

The rooms were rich. Mellow. Incredibly detailed. Painted arms of the Border families. Gleaming helms and cuirasses. Book bindings stamped in gilt.

There was a lot of old oak and it was red like a wood on fire. Bright red too for the walls of the armoury. But green in the drawing-room, a beautiful Chinese paper hand-painted with birds and blossoms.

It was the home of a man who loved animals and at one time had had twelve dogs. Landseer had painted Ginger, a bright-eyed black and tan terrier. Near it was another portrait, a cat called Hinse, savaged by Nimrod the staghound and touchingly epitaphed: 'My friend has killed my friend.' And here in the drawing-room, the Raeburn portrait showed Scott pensive with a deer-hound at his feet and a greyhound gazing into his face.

Victoria was entranced. She turned at last and found Dugald at her elbow.

'I came to look for you. I'm afraid the others are getting restive for their tea.'

Victoria glanced guiltily round the flowery green room. Lorraine and Magnus must have left her behind. For the moment she had forgotten their existence.

'Yes, they've gone,' Dugald corroborated, amused. 'No, don't apologise. It's rewarding. I'm always fascinated when I come here. And *I'm* not a writer.' It was the first serious recognition he had given her trade.

Pleasing, but she must not take advantage. They were going on to Dryburgh Abbey for tea. Seen from his side, it became a long and quite arduous day.

'I know you feel like champagne,' she said happily. 'But we've taken enough of your time. This was a brain-wave. Lorrie has loved it.' His head had jerked questioningly. Puzzled, she went on: 'I am right in thinking that it was mostly for her benefit?'

Dugald gave her a steady look. 'No, Victoria, you were the reason we came here. I hoped it would pleasure you.'

At first she could not believe her ears. Then joy was quenched by his face. It brought back the night before Lorraine's cancelled wedding when Michael had been torn between truth and compassion.

'I wanted to remove you before the announcement,' Dugald went on baldly. 'Seven was not the final winner. I withdrew him.'

The disappointment was acute. 'But why? I don't understand.'

'A technicality. He'll have his chance again.' He looked gently at her flushed face. 'You care too much, soldier. Don't get this out of proportion.'

'Surely *you* care?'

'No,' he said too quickly. 'I compromise. I always take the better of two evils.'

'Fair play means nothing, then?'

He answered slowly. 'Victoria, you are so engagingly young. Children and fools break themselves over trifles. Wise men bend.'

'*Was* this a trifle?' It came to her suddenly. 'Could it have been a suggestion that the judge was prejudiced?'

He surveyed her blandly. 'Knowing the lady personally, a suggestion of that nature could only be a trifle.'

'But that *was* it? My inadvertent conversation? Noticed by Jim Redfern and used as a threat?' Every word whipped up the colour in her cheeks.

'Not a threat, a joke. But in those hands a risk I couldn't take.'

'Everyone makes jokes.'

'Not everyone runs a slightly snide newspaper column. You have a short memory if you've forgotten what has gone before. The person who dumped that sheep-killer on you did so by his invitation.'

'That's ridiculous! Jim was only trying to help.'

'If you say so,' Dugald said calmly. 'I'd say Redfern may not have made the bullets, but he certainly fired them.'

'Are you suggesting someone wants me out?' Victoria was incredulous.

'It's a possibility you shouldn't disregard.'

'Oh, I don't disregard it,' she said icily. 'I've taken account of you from the start.'

'Me?' He gave a burst of laughter. 'You think that's the best I could do? If I wanted you out, girl, you'd be over the Border before you could blow on your porridge.'

The flames of love and fury make the same fire. It's a question of which is uppermost.

'You might find it more difficult than you imagine,' Victoria retorted. 'Threats and force leave me cold. I mind much more that you've made me look a fool. To say nothing of your friend who gave the award. I'm sure she's overjoyed at the inference in your backing down.'

'She's not, and neither am I. But she's taking her share of the blame for the indiscretion. Seven won hands down, he'll do it again. Reputations can't be won back so easily. For pity's sake see that. Don't go into the wildcat routine, it's sterile.' He paused with a certain odd look—a look that she found confusing, elemental and a little scaring. Today's quota of visitors to Abbotsford were dribbling out of the house. Here in the green drawing-room, in front of the strong Raeburn portrait, she was alone with a man as strong. 'Or is it?' The murmur was almost unheard as Dugald grasped her, pulled her against him and kissed her on the mouth. She intended to be cold and submissive; hurt and anger demanded a lack of response. He was kissing her only as a sort of revenge or a selfish demonstration of strength.

But hurt and anger were nowhere in the charge of feeling.

'I wouldn't have said force left you cold, my dear,' Dugald remarked with the gentleness of a spider.

# CHAPTER TEN

WHEN Magnus turned up for work on Monday, he followed Victoria round a corner and asked abruptly: 'Is this still on?'

She was impressed by his understanding. 'You mean because it wasn't your idea in the first place?'

'It was *his* suggestion,' Magnus said carefully. 'But I made jolly sure before I offered.' He stared into the distance, screwing up his eyes in a way she had noticed of late.

Magnus, it seemed, was a problem. Dugald had confided to Lorraine that he was not settling in at Baldougrie as well as they had hoped. And yet the partnership which his grandfather had bequeathed him had seemed an excellent arrangement. He had always been happy there when Walter Douglas was alive, accepting apparently without resentment that his own parents, both gifted scientists, had a life style of travel and research that effectively precluded staying for long in any one place.

Victoria did not pretend to understand, but she supposed this had always been the case with the 'greats' of any age and she thought only that it was a pity for their child's sake. Also she was not going to be hypocritical. Magnus would be a big loss. She told him so and was pleased to see his face light up.

That morning she met Mrs Bradley in the village.

'Have you time for a coffee?' Victoria invited on impulse. She was going to be intrusive, but she had got to know these neighbours well and somehow sensed they would not take offence at plain speaking.

Mrs Bradley said: 'I'd love it,' to the invitation and

they found a window table in the Grey Horse. It was a rather private table, overlooked only by a Scottish lion in pewter on a black wall shield.

Victoria fetched the two cups and saucers and a plate of biscuits. She looked at her guest doubtfully and then plunged in like the Number Seven.

'Mrs Bradley, this is a mean question. I hope you won't resent it. Your husband would have had a perfect right to object formally to my aunt's buildings. Did he?'

'Oh no.' The answer came so quickly that it had to be the truth. 'We wouldn't do such a thing,' Mrs Bradley affirmed. 'I don't say we didn't moan a bit, but that's all. I was sorry for her, believe me. I hope you *do*, dear. It certainly wasn't us.'

Victoria was shocked to discover how much she had counted on Mr Bradley's being the culprit. For nearly two weeks the thought had been a prop. Now the culprit had to be Dugald, there was no one else with motive.

Lorraine was disappointed that she did not come up for a second helping of a new mince dish which was spiced with chutney and curry and served with rice and lemon.

'You're doing too much, Vic. You need that break in Paris.'

It was little short of a miracle that Lorrie was so placid about taking charge on her own. She had even declined Ellen's offer to stay with her at night.

Just as well, perhaps, Victoria reflected as she drove to the clinic a week before her departure. Ellen's elderly cat, who had been on a course of injections from Craig, was again poorly and she would probably worry if she had to leave it alone.

This evening she had brought it back to the surgery, and the headshake she gave in response to Victoria's inquiry was answer enough.

'It is not that I do not know what I should do, it is just that I am not brave,' she said tremulously. 'Oh, indeed, it is easy to see your aunt is not here.'

Elizabeth Elliott had always been compelling when an animal needed release.

Ellen raised the lid of the basket and Victoria looked sadly inside. It was irritating that Craig was late and that Ellen should have to wait. Every second was taking its toll in heartbreak and indecision. She hoped he would make up Ellen's mind for her, quickly and kindly, and then take over. But Craig, she knew, was not a masterful person.

Aunt Elizabeth had been just that—a 'character', a dragon, an angel.

'He's getting old right enough,' Ellen said shakily. 'And she wouldn't want me to be saying no when I should be saying yes. "Come on now, Ellen," she'd say. "We never died a winter yet."'

Victoria drew a breath. 'Then leave him. I'll do the rest.' She put her hand on Ellen's and pressed it. Dugald's housekeeper looked her thanks. She had no words as she hurried out of the room.

Victoria had not seen Craig since the dog show and was half afraid he might cut up rough over her refusal to go to Dundee. However, he came in humming, and said merely that she had missed a good night. He looked Ellen's cat over and suggested another injection. 'It's only buying time, but she's besotted with it.'

It struck Victoria that this had happened before. Ellen's hopes had been raised and the cat had suffered on.

'Craig, it's time *now*. She knows it.'

His light blue eyes glinted. 'All right, give it here.

'Happy now?' he asked lightly as he left the room.

How serious he was, she knew not, but he had put the onus back on her shoulders. How right had she been?

And what would happen next? Victoria had come a long way since her first squeamishness, but this cat was about to die in her arms and she was alone and ignorant and scared.

The door opening behind her was a welcome sound. Craig must have had a change of heart. 'Can you stay, Craig, *please*! I don't know what to do,' she said falteringly.

'You're doing fine,' Dugald's deep voice replied.

His hand took her arm above the elbow.

He had met Ellen on her way home but had been unable to persuade her to get into the car. 'She wanted to be by herself, but I thought as I was passing this way I'd look in and set her mind at rest.'

Victoria was to realise afterwards that he was taking her own mind off what was happening, but indeed when she did look down there was nothing fearsome or repellent. Just a sleepy black and white cat blinking up at her and occasionally licking the tip of its nose.

'When you see that, it's nearly over,' Dugald said softly. He stroked the black head. 'Ellen will be grateful to you.'

'Craig was too busy to stay.' Defending Craig seemed to have become a habit.

'Yes,' Dugald said drily.

Two minutes later he took the cat gently from her arms.

'That was brave, soldier *beg*. Are you all right?' The Gaelic '*beg*' was that much more endearing than the English 'little'.

'Fine, thanks. I'm glad you were here.'

'Care to come to the Horse for a brandy?'

She shook her head. 'No, I mustn't. They'll need me at the clinic.'

'I'm sure they will,' he agreed quietly. 'Heart is a commodity in short supply these days.'

The words lay warmly in Victoria's consciousness for the rest of the clinic hour. The issue between Dugald Douglas and herself remained, but he was a chivalrous opponent. And perceptive. Craig had not absorbed one iota of her feelings. He could be fun, but in other ways he was porous.

Comparisons, however, were futile and when Craig asked her in for a drink at the close of surgery she did not refuse. There were things to discuss about next week, when she would be away.

'Paris, eh?' Craig gave a whistle of envy. 'Is this the thin end of the wedge?'

'More commonplace than that. It's bread and butter.' A long-standing assignment and a lucrative one. She was determined to fulfil it.

'Mind if I talk to you like a Dutch uncle?' He settled himself into a chair. 'You might be well advised to think again about Wild Heart. You've had it a few weeks now and I must admit ...' The pause was delicate. 'Well, tonight you went positively green about the gills. Candidly, sweetie, it needs a tough old bird like your aunt.' He went on to add quickly, 'No offence. Take it as a compliment.'

It was depressing, the more so because he had always encouraged her.

'And remember,' he was now saying earnestly, 'I'm here to help still. Whatever you decide. If you stay, well and good, if you don't I'll keep my ears to the ground for a purchaser and I'll get rid of the stock for you. No trouble at all.'

'Don't!' Victoria begged. 'That's what bothers me most.'

She had to be sensible, of course. They now had about twenty inmates and not all were house pets like Hairylegs, the Cat and Tango. Those three she could not part with, especially Tango.

The kitten was a home-lover; he never rambled like Cat and the others. He watched for her at the window and met her with a curl of joy. When he played he slapped with a flat paw. He had a little simpering face and his purr never stopped. In vogue cats were svelte and neurotic. Tango lying on his back was the shape of a kipper and he had no tricks. He just loved his tummy, and Cat, Victoria and Lorraine. He was a darling.

'You'll think me daft,' Victoria said slowly, 'but Tango is very important in the scheme of things. I can't see Wild Heart without him.'

'You *are* daft,' Craig told her, smiling. 'But neither can I see Wild Heart without you. Unless, of course, you'd consider a swop. This place isn't bad.'

Victoria gaped. 'Now wait a minute, Craig. What are you suggesting?'

'I can't believe my ears, but I think I'm suggesting you marry me.'

'It certainly sounded like some form of cohabiting! But breathe again. I didn't hear it.'

'Will you hear it the next time?'

He could not be serious. Yet for once he sounded it. Victoria felt confused—and touched. 'Let's not cross bridges. As you say, you've taken yourself by surprise.' She paused, never more conscious of the charm which from the first had attracted her. 'But thank you all the same. And for the offer of help. I'm sorry for being niggly over Ellen. Perhaps Lorrie is right—I do need a break.'

Arrangements had now been concluded and she was flying from Glasgow on Monday, returning the following Saturday.

'Stay longer if you want,' Lorraine offered. 'A holiday would do you good.'

'It might if someone else paid for it.' Victoria sometimes had qualms when she looked ahead. 'Or for us come the long dark winter.' She regretted the joke when she saw Lorraine wearing the old anxious look. 'Sorry. Not true. I'm going to get that book off the ground before Christmas if you'll mind the store again while I do some research in London.'

'Yes—well, we'll talk about it again.' It could not have been imagination that Lorraine looked restive. 'Meanwhile Dugald wants you to have dinner with him before you go. Tomorrow if that suits. He said it was a long-standing commitment.'

Aunt Helen had always operated on the maxim 'Better safe than sorry'. This was one time when Victoria agreed with it. The fewer encounters she had with Dugald the better for peace of mind. This one, however, seemed unavoidable.

'What are you wearing?' she asked casually. The blank look called for a repeat of the question. 'At Baldougrie. Tomorrow. What are you wearing?'

'I'm not going,' Lorraine said lightly. 'He did ask me, but I said no.'

As Victoria stared she grew edgy. 'Don't look at me like that. There's nothing wrong. I just want an early night.'

'I suppose you're washing your hair?' Victoria inquired sarcastically. 'Come off it, Lorrie. You must have a reason. You haven't quarrelled with Dugald?'

'Of course not. And I haven't got a headache. I can see you're going to ask. I just fancy staying at home— there are millions of things to do. Dugald understands that. I don't see why you can't.'

A slightly stunned Victoria accepted that she would have to. It was exactly the manner in which she herself had got out of dates in the past. Good in one way to see Lorrie able to handle herself. But not good in the certainty that something must be amiss. Her mind went back guiltily to the drawing-room in Abbotsford House when Dugald's lips had awakened new depths in her. Had her face betrayed her when they rejoined the others? Had Lorraine suspected it and been hurt?

It was a bitter thought, but everything seemed to endorse it. On Saturday her sister was more edgy and less like herself than ever.

It should have been possible to reassure her. A flame had spurted out of the rock of anger—heaven knows why—and then it had died. 'That was all Lorrie,' Victoria's thoughts ran desperately. 'He doesn't even like me, he thinks I'm mad.'

But a wall seemed to have come between them.

She said only: 'I'm sure I won't be late, but don't wait up,' and went out to the car.

As she neared the castle, she found herself following another car. It stopped at the main gates and the driver got out and tried to open them. When he failed to do so, he shrugged his shoulders, laughed, got into his car again and drove on.

Victoria dropped back. By the time she drove into the stable yard, the occupants of the other car were parking their vehicle.

Tonight, as always, the influence of Baldougrie was strong. Turret shapes against the grape blue sky. Archways and cobbles. The Hanoverian head of Dugald's grey horse looking over the door of his box.

Victoria took off her driving shoes, eased into heeled T-strap sandals and stood up with a swish of skirt. She had dressed with care—a long emerald green pinafore with a nipped-in waist, a bold print silky shirt in royal and the same bright green. A vivid rose lipstick and a chain and chunky pendant of Celtic silver. Two silver bangles on her right wrist. Her hair freshly set. and brushed to a deep silken gold.

She threw her stole over her arm and walked towards the archway that led to the front of the castle.

The couple from the other car looked back and waited for her. An elderly pair, discreetly well dressed, they were just the sort of friends Dugald would have, and Victoria liked them on sight.

The man opened the conversation. 'I presume we're bound for the same place. Always amuses me to see those gates kept shut. I think we must tell our host Snow White is dead.' His hand went out. 'Rod McWilliam. This is my wife Sheila.'

Victoria supposed that some day someone would explain why Baldougrie closed its gates. 'Victoria Elliott. How do you do?'

It was a simple statement; it had a surprise effect.

'Elliott?' Mr McWilliam echoed. 'You did say Elliott?' He chuckled. 'Well, that's a good one. It seems the joke is on me.'

Victoria opened her mouth to say she didn't understand, but at that moment Dugald came out to meet them. He put his arms round Sheila McWilliam and gripped Rod's hand. It was good to see them, he said warmly. It had been far too long.

Victoria had never seen Dugald like this before; it was riveting. So, in this setting of ancient splendour, was his kilt. It was backed by the blue herringbone jacket, a light blue silk tie, spotless white cuffs, a signet ring.

She was content to be overlooked because beside these old friends she was not of the least importance. But after only seconds her turn came. Dugald took both her hands and grasped them warmly.

'Hullo, my dear, I'm so glad you could come,' he said.

The party was enormously enjoyable. It had been arranged at short notice—Dugald had learned only the day before that Rod and Sheila would be in the vicinity —but Ellen had coped with amazing skill and panache.

The first course, thin brown bread with either

smoked salmon or liver pâté, was served on a trolley in the hall beneath the portrait of the young Cameronian officer. The main dish was roast turkey with cranberry sauce and stuffing that contained ground almonds, sultanas and lemon. Dugald opened a bottle of Liebfraumilch Madonna. For sweet there were poached mandarins dashed in Cointreau.

'You don't do so badly,' Victoria said teasingly.

'But he needs a wife,' Sheila McWilliam put in unexpectedly. 'And he's doing nothing about it,' she mourned.

Dugald glanced up from his plate and smiled at her. 'How do you know?' he murmured.

A joke, perhaps, but it posed an instant question. Lorraine? The course of true love was notoriously uneven. Lorrie's absence tonight could signify just that. Stress. A temporary rift. Even a feeling of unpreparedness and panic.

Lorrie, how could you? Victoria questioned; last time was different, but *this time how could you not know?*

The tide of conversation was absorbing. The McWilliams lived in Edinburgh and were in close touch with Dugald's mother. She had opened a boutique in Edinburgh some years ago and since her husband's death lived and worked there full-time. During the Festival Mrs Douglas put on a fashion show in Baldougrie Castle. This year it was being held on August the thirty-first.

'A date for your diary,' Dugald remarked, glancing at Victoria. 'You're getting a free ticket, so we'll be looking for a tremendous write-up.'

Another time the spotlight fell on Magnus, who was seated at the other end of the table facing his uncle and looking tall and tapered in a smart lounge suit. To begin with he had been as monosyllabic as ever, but

Sheila's affectionate banter was irresistible. Victoria pricked her ears when she heard: 'And what about that pretty nurse who asked you to write to her?' Magnus, it seemed, had been hospitalised in Edinburgh for some weeks in the early summer following a car crash when a school friend's mother had taken him out for the day.

And now it came back to Victoria that Dugald had once referred to 'M. McAlester' having gone to Edinburgh to see his doctor. She hoped everything was all right. She hoped it fervently and she thought it dreadful that his parents should have been so far away. Christmas Island, Magnus was now saying, was their present base.

At the coffee stage Dugald confided that he had had talks about the establishing of a guide dog training unit at Baldougrie. He had plenty of space and he thought it would be a simple matter to convert some property into a hostel for the human trainees.

'Ay, you're a humanitarian like your father,' Rod declared. 'Good luck, lad. Many folk will be the richer if you can pull it off.'

'But you really *will* need a wife then,' Sheila put in merrily.

Dugald looked annoyed. 'I don't think my matrimonial prospects are in question. If it eventuates there'll be trained staff.'

'But maybe not with the right name!' Rod was incorrigible as well as not making sense, though to judge from Dugald's rigid expression it had a meaning, and a most unpalatable one.

And at that moment Victoria glanced down the table and saw something as incomprehensible and even more troubling. It was the utter misery on Magnus's face.

When the meal ended the men went off to the kennels, Magnus managed to detach himself and Victoria followed Sheila back to the hall.

Someone, presumably Ellen, had switched on a small side lamp. A fire burned brightly, lighting the carved mantel. She noticed for the first time that a shield bearing the McAlester arms hung opposite the Douglas insignia. The latter with its crown and heart had become familiar.

There was also a photograph. Victoria tried to keep her eyes away from it, but suddenly Sheila rose and brought it across for her to see. There was no doubt as to the identity of the subject. Beautiful cheekbones, a winged mouth, challenging eyes, Grecian styled shining hair. Very, very lovely as she had always known she would be.

Victoria's eyes lifted in a question there was no need to ask.

'You've heard the story?' Sheila McWilliam did not seem surprised.

'It's been haunting me,' Victoria replied.

'I think it had that effect on us all at first, but it's a long time ago now and life has gone on, as it should do. Dugald is not the kind to let grief curdle him.'

And you, you nice person, are telling me this because you think I care for him, Victoria thought dully. Well, it was true. She couldn't deny it. The ghastly question was how obvious she had made it.

Carefully, she brought the conversation round to Magnus. They should call a spade a spade, Sheila declared; Dugald's sister had never wanted a child, she had made it clear from the beginning that he must not interfere with her work. 'Which I think he has always accepted. He's resilient and quite unsentimental.'

'And very unhappy. I'm sure of it,' Victoria said flatly.

Sheila looked momentarily troubled but not convinced. Then Victoria saw her glance at her watch. They had to talk, she said briskly, and time was getting on. She must get Rod on the road before too late.

'I had no idea we were going to meet you, and I want to say this. If you ever want to close Wild Heart, I'll guarantee all your animals a good home. Our new place will be opening in a month. I hope you'll drive over and take a look at it, ask for Willie Saunders. He's going to be in charge. I've been meaning to write to you ever since I read that article in the *Argus*. It seemed a way we could help.'

'You're Dugald's friends on the Animal Welfare Council?' Victoria asked slowly. 'I didn't know.'

Sheila nodded. 'I met your aunt once. She had very striking eyes, I remember. And I don't think anyone would dispute that, however she got Wild Heart from Walter Douglas, the end justified the means.'

Victoria blinked. She told herself to keep calm. It had, after all, always been there—the missing link. How had Aunt Elizabeth raised the money for a property like Wild Heart. 'We assumed she bought it,' she said.

'Oh no, my dear.' Sheila McWilliam gave Victoria's hand a pat. 'She won it. She beat him at chess.'

As the McWilliams' car swung out of the courtyard with Sheila's hand fluttering at the window Dugald dropped his arm. 'It seems we have got to talk.'

If she had needed confirmation of her fears it was here. The face was set, the voice studiedly calm. There was no trace of the man who not three hours ago had greeted them with such warmth.

Clearly the dinner had been another ploy to persuade her to relinquish Wild Heart. And it had misfired. Rod and Sheila had scented a romance. That double talk, those jokes, their kindly looks—Victoria wished she could stop thinking of them. So wrong, so blushmaking—and twice as bad for Dugald, who was probably concerned about Lorraine.

Back in the hall, he came straight to the point. 'You were placed in an awkward position. I apologise. They are very old friends and I'm afraid my welfare has become almost as great an obsession as their animal homes. I hope you can understand and pardon.'

'I don't think either is necessary.' She hoped the finer point would not escape him. A look from the deep set eyes suggested that it had not.

'The gates,' he began as though weighing his words, 'are historical with the inevitable dash of romance. At the end of the fourteenth century the Douglases talked the Elliotts into joining them on the Border in Liddesdale. From then on the two clans were friends and allies. But some time in the eighteenth century a Grizel Elliott, betrothed to one of my ancestors, ran away with a Maxwell just before their wedding. My ancestor closed the gates of Baldougrie as a monument to his grief and when the castle was rebuilt my great-grandfather regrettably revived the gimmick. The gates remain closed till the families marry again.' He stopped and there was a pause.

Victoria, looking at the tinge of pink on his cheekbones, decided he was thinking of Lorraine. Again she was sorry for the invidious position into which he had been forced.

'Knowing you,' she said lightly, 'there's a more practical reason.'

'Indeed. Thirty or forty of them—all liable to rush out on the main road and get killed.'

She had induced a breath of fresh air into a turgid atmosphere, but suddenly she herself was cold. She held out her hands to the grate, thinking that in these days a coal and log fire was something of a rarity. It brought comfort and an old, old sense of cosiness. She needed both, so she kneeled there for a minute or two, not speaking.

And Dugald watched her, but this she did not see.

'Rod and Sheila *were* the friends you mentioned to Lorrie? The ones who would take the animals if I sold you Wild Heart? I can see now why you wanted me to meet them.'

'I wanted you to know that the way is there if you need it; I felt you should see them rather than take my word. They may be garrulous, but they're a marvellous pair. You should see some of the homes they run.'

She nodded. She knew it would be true.

'When you go to Paris, little one,' Dugald said quietly, 'you may not want to come back—at least not to Wild Heart. This was never your world.' She felt his hands close gently on her shoulders.

It was the way to end all possible doubt as to her feelings.

'I have thought about that. Of course there's Lorrie . . .'

'I don't think you should worry about her.'

When she turned her head he looked at her from the carved armchair, his face very kind. 'No one is suggesting you should go, unless for your own sake. You have confounded us, soldier *beg*, you have done so well.'

It was almost unbearable. 'Dugald.' Again she twisted round to look up at him. 'Why did you never tell me how Aunt Elizabeth got Wild Heart from your father?'

The hands on her shoulder tensed. 'The de'il take it! Can Sheila never keep her mouth shut?'

Victoria did not think Sheila should be blamed. It was right she should know. She had been given something to which she had no right. Sheila had told the story jokingly; Aunt Elizabeth had met Walter Douglas at an animal welfare meeting and the acquaintance had grown. She was a personality, and he liked that. She had asked to rent a cottage on his land, he had proposed a game of chess with Wild Heart as the stake.

But it was absurd. If Walter Douglas had chosen to be quixotic there was a moral obligation not to accept. A gift of that kind was pure fantasy.

'My father was like that,' Dugald said.

'But *she* wasn't. At least, not when I last saw her.' It all came frettingly back to that. The neglect that had not seen bravery turn into eccentricity. 'Why didn't you contest it? Why didn't you send for me?'

'It was best not spoken about.' His face was poker-straight. 'My father felt the disgrace of being beaten. Especially by a woman!'

Victoria was to wonder afterwards what came over her. At the time she was just too weary to argue or get up. So she stayed kneeling with his hand against her cheek.

'I am so ashamed,' she said.

# CHAPTER ELEVEN

CRAIG called unexpectedly on Sunday night. He offered to drive Victoria to Glasgow and was disappointed when she would not accept.

'But why should you?' Victoria argued. It would take almost the whole day and he had a practice to look after.

'Because I like your company. I'm the guy who asked to marry you, remember.'

'But we thought—not seriously,' she reminded him.

'Very seriously. For your money, of course.' He planted a kiss expertly on her cheek.

'I'm sorry. You've caught me in a rotten mood,' she apologised. 'Something has come up about Wild Heart.'

Craig was a good listener. He seemed to know that she must get it off her chest and he gave undivided attention. When she had finished he held her hand and put forth his solution.

'You can't give it back to him, honey; you can try, but he won't have it, mark my words. Put the place on the market, marry me and we'll cope together. I'm used to this sort of thing.'

Ironically, it steadied her. She too was used to coping. The days of helpless womanhood were over, but Craig meant well and his kindness touched her.

It was provoking that Tango was afraid of him and made it so obvious. The kitten was big enough now for castration and she dreaded it. Foolish in the extreme, but she could not shake herself out of it.

'It's routine,' Craig told her. 'Bring him down some morning and you'll have him back by teatime.'

She would do so, she resolved, as soon as she got home.

The five days in Paris passed quickly. She was busy and she met old friends. One night she rang home and Lorraine sounded happy and confident. Whatever had had her on edge during Saturday had obviously been forgotten. Victoria replaced the receiver, immensely relieved.

She had enjoyed the return to her own scene, but it had not disengaged her. She had thought constantly of Wild Heart and on Saturday as the land beneath the jet became Scotland it gave her a thrill of pride. The tilting fields were as gold as the whisky they would make; there were lockets of blue water and green hills cutting up the arcs of sky.

Sitting there and drinking it all in Victoria had no doubts as to what she wanted to do. She wanted to stay.

To her astonishment Craig was waiting at the airport. He made light of the distance, but she knew it was a round trip of a hundred and thirty miles.

Since the night he had put down Ellen's cat, he seemed to have lost a lot of his impatience. He had been kind last Sunday and again today. She looked affectionately at the smooth fair head and wondered why on earth she didn't love him and was it true that the best marriages were those gone into with eyes wide open and feet firmly on the ground.

After all what good would it do to spend her life crying for the moon?

The car slowed down a little and Craig looked round at her. 'I can't go any further without telling you,' he said. 'A rotten thing has happened. The kitten ran off. I had it down in the surgery, and it got away. I'm damned sorry.'

It had been intended as a kindness. Had all gone well she would have come home to find the castration over.

Craig knew her stupid feelings about even the preliminaries, starving a kitten that was always breakfast-crazy, calling it and shutting it into a basket. So, in a way, it was her fault for being over-protective.

She had to be objective because if she let herself think of Tango's door-stop eyes and his funny little 'pushed in' mouth she would have been in tears.

'Well, at least he's not dead. When—did it happen?'

It had happened yesterday and everyone had searched, Lorraine, Magnus, the village children, even Craig himself. He was desperately upset, and his self-reproaches made her feel that she was looking at a new Craig and a much more endearing one.

It had suddenly become a topsy-turvy world.

Lorraine was equally distressed, blaming herself where there was no cause.

'Oh, Vic, I feel awful about this, you were so fond of him.'

'Don't talk as though he's dead. Perhaps he'll find his way home,' Victoria said stoutly. It was something to cling to, but she hadn't much hope. There were many hazards—dazzling headlights, foxes, gamekeepers, even thieves. Tango was growing his coat, it had a close silky pile and it was the red of barley sugar. Anyone would love him, and he loved everyone except Craig.

It did no good to remember how he had behaved last Sunday evening, creeping on his belly to the nearest hiding place.

On Tuesday after the clinic, Craig brought up the future. 'It's been over a week, love, have you thought?'

Victoria had not gone to Paris exactly to think; she had had a full and tiring schedule and she said so gently. 'As a matter of fact I got this urge on the plane coming home to stay in Wild Heart. Maybe I have no right to it, maybe I should insist on Dugald taking it back ...'

'Oh, that's nonsense. It was a free gift, and you know she'd hate him to have it, him above all.'

That was the terrible thing. It was a plausible argument, the only one that really should sway her.

'Compromise,' Craig suggested. 'Let me get rid of it for you, and then if you don't want to leave us, you can always take up your option on me.'

'You say that,' Victoria said wonderingly, 'as if you thought I'd marry you just for a place to live.'

'No, I don't think that,' he returned flatly. 'I've never been good at pipe dreams.' He added that he had spent half an hour that morning searching for Tango in derelict buildings once owned by the Forestry Commission.

Victoria tried to express her feelings over a shandy in the Grey Horse. She had decisions to make and losses to face up to; she had always found that time solved most things and she wanted it to happen that way. He must not consider himself bound in any way. And he was not obligated to continue looking for Tango.

'For Pete's sake think of some way I can help. It'll make me feel better,' Craig said as he dropped her at Wild Heart. He had already volunteered to take both Lorraine and herself to Baldougrie for the Fashion Show, brushing aside decisively any suggestion that they could use their own transport.

There was something different about Lorraine. Victoria was remorseful for not noticing it before, but since Saturday all her anxiety had been for the kitten. The pain was controllable now and she had eyes for other people again.

Her sister had never looked fitter. Her face was tanned, her bones no longer showed and the larder shelves were stacked with homemade jam. Headaches seemed a thing of the past and most days she woke Victoria with a cup of tea. She did so the next morning, and stared when she heard of Craig's arrangement to escort them to Baldougrie.

'But we don't need him—I thought I'd told you. Dugald is sending a car.' It was said, Victoria noted, as though it was the most natural thing in the world. And doubtless it would be for the girl Dugald was going to marry. She was appalled by the envy that licked her up as she dressed. But hating herself did no good. The only real antidote was work.

She buckled her belt, brushed her hair, ran downstairs and threw a leg over her chair. 'Well, mate, you've had your trials. Will you do it again? A week, a month, say, till Christmas?'

Lorraine was fetching the coffee. She stopped short with the jug still in her hand. She was as red as a beetroot.

'I'm terribly sorry, Vic. I can't promise. And don't ask me to explain—please. Not just for the moment.

'I hate not telling you,' she added. 'But I will quite soon—tomorrow or the next day.'

Victoria's gaze went over the flushed face and Lorraine's dark blue glowing eyes. 'I think—I'm very happy for you,' she said softly.

'And I'm in your debt.' Poise was one of the new things about Lorraine. 'Yours and Aunt Elizabeth's.'

It was the day of the Fashion Show at Baldougrie and Magnus reported that things were 'up in a heap'. There were electricians putting up floodlights, and caterers driving Ellen 'up the pole'. His grandmother had arrived from Edinburgh and Dugald was back from a dog show in Aberdeen. Some dancers were also coming and musicians.

'It's a bit boring,' he concluded. 'But I suppose everyone to his taste.'

'What's your taste, Magnus? Dog training?' Victoria asked daringly.

Sometimes providence has a way of giving clues which are not apparent at the time. Magnus's eyes stared straight into hers and she thought how beautiful they were, wide and pansy dark. He said woodenly: 'I'll have to wait and see.'

Victoria walked Hairylegs and two of the other dogs briskly through the glen. They negotiated the primitive stone stile and climbed up the brae. She thought about Magnus and about their timetable for the evening, which included hair appointments in the village. Of Dugald she had vowed not to think at all, but this was not very successful, because just where the bracken stopped at the top of the hill she all but bumped into him.

'Hullo there,' he said promptly. 'I was on my way to you.' He wanted to let them know that he would call at seven-thirty. It was an hour earlier than the time on the ticket, but that way they could all have a quiet drink before the crowd arrived. 'All right?' He seemed to take it for granted. 'Then I won't come any further. The homestead is under attack from all sides.'

Lorraine had said: 'Dugald is sending a car.' Victoria had assumed one of his assistants would come and she had had no notion they would be asked to arrive early. She was dreadfully disappointed, she would have loved the opportunity of meeting his mother. Though, of course, she was not the one Mrs Douglas would most want to see.

'I'm sure that will be fine for Lorrie. Actually, Craig is coming for me.'

'Craig?' Dugald's brows knit. 'Craig Maxwell? But you knew ...'

Victoria shook her head. 'Lorrie is sure she told me

we were getting a lift, but I'm afraid I was so upset over Tango it didn't register.'

Dugald had not heard about the kitten; he made an impatient comment about 'Magnus living in a world of his own'. 'I'm sorry,' he added. 'You were very fond of it. What does Craig have to say?'

'He's desperately sorry. It wasn't his fault.'

'Oh! I should have thought he'd find it difficult to put the blame anywhere else.'

She felt in duty bound to defend the absent Craig. 'I mean it was an accident. It could have happened to anyone.'

'It has never happened in my experience with any vet.' Dugald was firm. She couldn't guess at his thoughts, but she had a feeling they were deep. His eyes had narrowed almost as though he felt pain. 'You're either very forgiving or very fond.'

Until that morning at breakfast Victoria had not realised how much she needed Craig as an escort for tonight. Everyone would know very soon about Dugald and Lorraine, and she could not bear them to say: 'I always thought the young sister was fond of him.'

'Can you put him off?' Dugald asked bluntly.

'No, I don't think so. I'm sorry.' She tried not to see the coldness in his face.

The temptation to give in was a big one, but Craig had been kind and she had a feeling he would take exception to a change of plan. Bewilderingly, it did not seem trivial to Dugald either.

'It's your decision,' he said curtly, and turned away.

When Victoria had arrived back last month after her tour, she had gone bag and baggage to Aunt Helen's house and the easiest thing, when she had been summoned to Scotland, had been to sling anything into the boot of the car. She had far more clothes than she would otherwise have brought. It had been the opposite with Lorraine. She had expected to be away no longer than a week and she had had no heart then for Scotland or anywhere else. She had very little in her case and nothing remotely suitable for a party, but she had gone into Selkirk during the week and purchased a long skirt.

'It will do well enough with a blouse,' she had said, displaying it to Victoria.

This morning, walking home after the conversation with Dugald, Victoria knew suddenly that it would not do at all. Lorraine must make a favourable impression, and Dugald's mother was a doyen in the field.

'So you're going to wear "The Find",' she informed her sister. 'Thank goodness I never got round to chopping it.'

'The Find' had come from Mexico. She had come by it honestly but at greatly reduced cost. It had all the earmarks of its country, pintucked beige cotton, ribbon, snow-white insertions and snow-white lace edging. It did not bother her that it had been made for a tall girl; she would enjoy working out how best to shorten it. But she had not got round to it yet.

It looked magical on Lorraine. There was a saintly look to the long frosty cuffs and a festive air to the turquoise ribbons. She went off protesting but obviously pleased with the effect. Victoria took care to remain out of sight until the car had driven away. She knew she could not avoid Dugald for the whole evening, but their meeting would be easier in a crowd.

Craig arriving late blamed it on the car. As they got under way he hardly gave her a second glance. All the talk was about the engine. The garage had done something to it that morning, but it still didn't feel right.

Victoria sympathised and let things be. Cars could be very frustrating.

'I'm not having much luck lately, am I?' he muttered.

'Please stop worrying over Tango. I mean it. We've done all we can.'

'And you can leave it at that? I envy you.' He frowned irritably at the noise the car was making. 'I thought you'd close up the whole shebang if he went. You once said that.'

'Yes.' She remembered the conversation. 'But I won't. Even if he'd been a person I'd know life had to go on.'

And who am I really talking about, she wondered, Tango or Dugald?

A hundred yards from their destination the car coughed wearily to a standstill. Not all Craig's efforts could make it budge. In the end he gave up ill-humouredly and they walked the rest of the way.

Baldougrie was en fête. The effect of the floodlights was theatrical. Disembodied silver battlements. Arms a shell of colour on the wall. The hall with a space cleared for the dancers and the musicians tuning up in the minstrels' gallery. And the drawing-room, which to date Victoria had never seen. The dust sheets had been removed and eggshell blue upholstery came to life against the white walls.

Tonight it was a sort of reception area. Drinks were being served and she could see Lorraine in a group which included Dugald. She had only a moment to note how utterly right her sister looked before Dugald detached himself and came down the room.

He was in evening dress. Stiff white lace, velvet doublet, hose in the tartan of his kilt, that tartan sufficiently picturesque for all occasions.

'Welcome,' he said smilingly. 'We were getting nervous. But I suppose good results take their time to produce.' His hand seemed for a second to tighten its hold. 'It was worth waiting for,' he told her softly.

Although to herself she made no bones about it—he was making amends for the morning's brusqueness and

welcoming her into the family as his future sister-in-law
—the compliment made her glow.

There was a blurred excitement about the next few minutes.

She had pictured Dugald's mother as tall and stately with smart white hair; in fact Peg Douglas could have passed for an elder sister. She was dark with a gamine haircut. Crowsfeet added spice to her face. She wore a long russet overdress, a toning cream top and a necklace of knotted gold cords.

'Victoria Elliott,' she said, lightly holding Victoria's hand. 'This is an honour—and I mean that. I've read and admired you for years.'

They had so much in common that Victoria felt guilty at stealing Lorraine's limelight. She reassured herself that her sister looked perfectly happy and followed her hostess to what Peg Douglas laughingly termed 'the press box'.

The show, unlike those she had written up last week in Paris, was laid on for the middle range budget. Peg liked the unusual, tabards and slipovers, boiler suits, Aztec-printed rain-hats, but she made room for the pretty clothes as well. Victoria, jotting busily, noted mix and match flower prints, a flounced and strapless sundress and charming peasanty cottons with lace-edged headscarves and frilly-hemmed petticoats. There was a lot of knitwear, mostly in random wool or with bright patterns and for the classics lovely straight legged trousers and a blue raincoat with stitching and a panelled yoke.

'Now you and I are going to have our supper,' Peg announced when the models had finally left the cat walk. 'It's maddening having such a short time.' She was leaving first thing in the morning, hurrying back to the boutique.

Victoria looked round for Lorraine and saw that

Dugald was looking after her. Craig was talking earnestly to an elderly lady. She felt guilty about him. He had come on her account and she was sure he wasn't enjoying himself.

So many people set the ball rolling by telling her they had known Aunt Elizabeth that it was refreshing when Peg said bluntly that she had never met her. 'But then I'm not often here. Walter always understood, Dugald does too. When the time comes I shall be the ideal mother-in-law, never underfoot.' She smiled.

It seemed a pity and Lorraine would undoubtedly think so too.

'A little sometimes, I would hope,' Victoria said diffidently.

'You make that quite tempting,' Peg returned. 'Come and see me in Edinburgh. Stay with me I mean. We could go shopping together.'

Victoria would have liked to take her up on it. She had warmed to Peg Douglas from the first.

Dugald's mother spoke about herself with candour: 'You must never blame my daughter for wanting to lead her own life. She gets it from me. Even when my husband was alive I was here very little—and yet we loved each other. It's a funny unfeminine thing, but I can't take root in one place.'

Victoria saw nothing funny about it. She understood perfectly. '"Come forth, the sky is wide,"' she said softly. It was a quotation from John Buchan, and Dugald's mother looked a little startled and then went on with it.

'"There is a road which leads to the moon and it has no end, but it is a braw road—who will follow it?" You too? Yes, I suppose so. I should have guessed.' She looked at Victoria as though she were trying to say something else. It was a rather sad look and for a moment Victoria thought of explaining how the flight path into Glasgow Airport last Saturday had suddenly become as braw a road as any she had travelled to date.

'Have you heard about Caroline?' The unexpected question made her jump. 'The girl Dugald was engaged to?'

'Yes.' Caroline, Victoria was thinking. It was a suitable name.

'This will sound hard,' Peg said carefully, 'but it might have been sadder still if she'd married him. Don't misunderstand. I was fond of Caroline and I knew exactly what she feared when she refused him so many times. Of course she lost her clear sightedness as time went on, or rather as he wore her down. He was very young then, but he's known for a long time—I'm quite sure of this, Victoria—that it wouldn't have worked. You must build on rock, not sand, if you want it to last. I don't know if that helps at all,' she added offhandedly, 'but I wanted to say it.'

It should, of course, have been said to Lorraine, but Victoria could see the difficulty. Lorrie was with Dugald as she had been all evening and obviously the subject could not have been raised in front of him. But it had been generous of Peg to have thought of it. And there was no doubt she did feel immensely reassured.

'You two are looking very serious.' Dugald had crossed the room. 'I think they're starting the dancing. Can you tear yourselves away?'

'I'm sure Victoria can,' Peg said promptly. 'I'll follow you. I must have a word with the caterers before they go.'

Dugald took Victoria back into the hall. The musicians had struck up and thin sweet fiddling drifted from the gallery. Into this setting the dancers bounded, four smiling couples, pointing their toes and springing off the balls of their feet. They were not the kilted troupe Victoria had been expecting but something more uncommon. The men were in trunk hose and doublets, the girls in farthingales. The period was Elizabethan and they were dancing the galliard. Folk in the Borders, Dugald explained straight-faced, had always been more civilised than the wild Highlanders. 'Though I had better not let Magnus hear me,' he added, and glanced round.

Victoria followed hs gaze. Magnus was standing against a wall watching with narrowed eyes. It gave her an idea which she kept to herself.

As the dancers came to the end of their repertoire they threw the floor open to all who cared to join them. Dugald looked at Victoria, who was standing beside him starry-eyed. Her dress was remarkably like those of the girl dancers, high-necked, high-waisted and braided, but in some red and apricot all-over print like a *mille florets* paperweight. The long skirt was full and the bishop sleeves enormously so. It gave her dignity. Custom, he thought, would never stale the infinite variety of Victoria Elliott.

He asked courteously: 'May I have the pleasure?'

Victoria, taking her place opposite him, was at first very timid. Dugald astonished her. A man dancing the galliard has to leap in the air. He did this with agility, his kilt swirling. Bit by bit Victoria's restraint fell away. She had seen the dance once before at a village wedding in Spain, Dugald's eyes and his hands did the rest. She followed him gaily, the light catching her hair and the reds in her medieval dress.

When the music stopped she seemed to be the only one not expecting it. But there it was—the real dancers bowing and curtseying and a lot of clapping from the rest of the room. She stood hot-cheeked, making herself wind down. It was imperative because she knew that in another moment she and Dugald would have kissed. Not because he loved her, she realised, but because she was there and not hideously unattractive and he felt like it.

And the awful thing was how much she wanted it—even on those terms.

For a minute they seemed to be the only two in the room and then the struggle was over. He took her hand and raised it very gently to his lips.

'Did someone once say: "Never the hall such a galliard did grace?"'

No one seemed to have noticed her change of colour. Lorraine was Victoria's first fear, but she had never looked prettier or happier. Craig also seemed to have enjoyed himself. He had stayed with his elderly acquaintance almost the whole evening. She was a Mrs Glenloching who owned an estate near Baldougrie and had an amount of livestock including a herd of Ayrshires.

In a whispered conversation, Craig confided that the vet who had attended the estate for many years was about to retire. ' 'Nuff said!' he concluded, dropping Victoria a wink.

When the evening closed arrangements had to be made about transport. Dugald was driving Mrs Glenloching home and, naturally, Lorraine. When he heard about the mishap to Craig's car he said there would also be room for him and Victoria. It would be a pleasant drive by the Tweed with a moon to show it off, but if they preferred to go straight home he would get one of the lads to take them. Victoria chuckled to herself at Craig's instant disclaimer. He was still pursuing his changes with Mrs Glenloching's herd and would do so, she felt, till the last available minute. For her own part she was quite happy with the plan. It was a perfect night and the drive would be delightful.

Despite her years, Mrs Glenloching was a keen angler and still up to tackling sea trout, Scotland's liveliest game fish. The Tweed had some of the finest salmon in Western Europe, but apparently this was not the time for them. Just the same, she told them in a conspiratorial tone, there were salmon at the moment in Drummers' Pool.

'Get away!' Dugald exclaimed. 'Where did they come from?'

Mrs Glenloching did not know whether they were a freak run or some that had hung on from May and June, but they were quite big. MacNab, her keeper, had them under surveillance.

'Do I take that as a warning?' Dugald asked mischievously.

'I don't know when you ever did that, Dugald Douglas,' she retorted. 'But Willie MacNab was always so cracked about you he'd never let on.'

'How is he? I haven't seen him about lately.'

'Well enough. Getting old like his gaffer.'

'Now that I refuse to believe.' Dugald turned neatly into a driveway and Victoria realised that they had come to the end of the journey.

They didn't linger and were on the road again within five minutes. It was a quiet, empty night. The Tweed lay slightly below them, deep and still. An owl was up and calling against the moon. 'Drummers' Pool,' Dugald said with a reminiscent smile.

Suddenly he stopped the car and switched off engine and headlights. 'Ssh!' he warned sharply when Craig asked what was the matter. 'I thought I saw something. Over there.' He let himself quietly out of the car.

Victoria waited for Craig to join him, but Craig sat tight. It felt all wrong to sit in the car, so she got out.

'Don't come any further,' Dugald cautioned. 'It depends who they are.'

She took this to mean that if one or two of the

villagers were taking a fish Mrs Glenloching and her keeper would not want to know.

Dugald was on top of the rise looking down towards the water. Where Victoria could see nothing but inky darkness, she knew it meant much more to him. He was kin to this country, he could read it, hear it and even smell it. Now it was telling him what he wanted to know. As she watched he slid under the wire fence.

'I told you not to come any further. Get back in the car.'

She went reluctantly. Perhaps it was silly to be anxious, she couldn't help it. If he stumbled on an organised gang, he would be outnumbered and attacked. Craig sat peacefully, smoking and looking unmoved. Victoria knew he didn't consider it his business.

'It's so dark,' she fretted. 'You didn't see that slope.'

'You forget how often he's done it in the past,' Craig returned lazily.

Ten or fifteen minutes dragged by and she could bear it no longer. 'I'm going to see what's happening.'

'Don't be absurd,' Craig drawled.

Victoria got out of the car. The place where Dugald had gone down was too precipitous. She looked for an easier way and found it after some false starts.

'You're being silly, you know,' was Craig's last word.

'Vic, please be careful,' Lorraine had begged.

Dugald, Victoria thought, had not been careful. Something was going on that shouldn't, and that had been enough. She had to be at his side. It was as simple as that.

She found her footing at last on level ground. A minute was necessary to get her bearings. The Tweed, rippling under the moonlight, was low, the flat-topped boulders on which an angler might stand were dry. But there was no sign of people. Voices, however, were audible somewhere to her left. As she followed them, the river took a bend and went dark under the trees. Dark and, at a guess, deep. The bulge, she judged, was Drummers' Pool.

What happened next was confusing. A dark form carrying something like a spear seemed to come at her out of the undergrowth. As she drew back, another followed it. They went past without touching her and running hard. She moved uncertainly and felt herself grabbed and pushed. Next minute she was flat on her back. A third man was clattering down the bank after his companions, she heard an engine being started and then Dugald was standing over her. He had one of the men's weapons in his hand and the combination of spear, kilt and doublet made him, to fuddled eyes, a figure from the past. His voice, however, was unquestionably present day.

'*Are you daft?* I warned you to stay in the car!'

Victoria struggled to pick herself up. He gave her an impatient hand. 'What did you think you were doing? I told you to stay away.'

She had been prepared for a scolding, but not this grey, knifelike anger. 'Someone had to come. There was only one of you.'

'But not *you*.' Her sensitive nerves could take only contempt from his tone. 'I don't want *you* down here. *You—least of all!*'

# CHAPTER TWELVE

WHEN Lorraine brought the tea next morning, Victoria was already up and working at the notes she had taken at the Fashion Show.

'I wasn't sleepy,' she said when her sister began to scold.

In fact, she had hardly slept. A man will speak the truth under stress. Dugald had done just that. Later, of course, he had tried to cover it up. 'Now you're here, come and tear up your petticoat.'

The armed poachers had not been village lads, the van they had driven off in indicated that they had come a distance. But Dugald had not been first on the scene. The old keeper, Willie MacNab, had surprised the gang in the course of his patrol and had been assaulted and left lying half in and half out of the pool.

The next hour, in memory, was a lot of things. It was staying with the injured man while Dugald went for help. It was Lorraine, cool and calm, wiping away the blood with Craig's handkerchief. It was choking back the tears of reaction and trying to accept the facts. It was Dugald organising a stretcher party from the cottages on the estate and it was Craig unexpectedly noticing her expression and putting his arm around her.

She knew it suited Craig's plans to be conspicuous now that they were back at the house, but she had appreciated the kindness. Craig might have his faults, but his arm was warming and she had stayed close to him. If Dugald were to draw the wrong conclusion it really did not matter.

What had crystallised for her was the certainty that

she could not live permanently in Strathfin. In some ways leaving it would break her heart, but since meeting the McWilliams she had wondered constantly whether the animals' best interests did not lie with the new Home. Lorraine would certainly take Hairylegs with her, perhaps Cat as well. And Tango was gone. Victoria was sure she should have got over the loss of the kitten by now, but the truth was that she hadn't.

It was in a mood of despondency that she went out to feed the dogs. This was usually Magnus's chore, but with all the comings and goings at the castle he might not get away. She glanced across the scrubland past Charlie's field and saw Number Seven's yellow shape heading towards her. It was weeks since he had broken out of quarters and she was a little surprised. His slow rate of progress was also surprising. Seven was still apt to come at you like a thunderbolt.

And then she saw something orange in his mouth.

'Dead or alive,' she had prayed in the past few days. 'At least let me know.' The thing the dog was carrying looked very limp and she braced herself to face another truth.

Seven came trotting on. There was a pleased air about him. Not so about his burden. Suddenly Tango wanted to be put down. It was no way for the master of the house to return. He gave a wail of fury. It was the sweetest sound in the world.

The kitten was thin, draggled and exhausted. It seemed certain he had been trying to make his way home and had got as far as Baldougrie.

'And then he hitch-hiked,' Victoria told Magnus joyously.

Having fed the wanderer, and left him to sleep off his experiences, they had come up the glen with some of the other dogs. Magnus, Victoria decided, would have to know her thoughts about the future. In the past few weeks Wild Heart had depended on him more and more and it would be wrong to let him hear of its closure from a third party, even one as close as Dugald.

She chose her words carefully making no attempt to disguise her sorrow or the struggle the decision had cost.

'I suppose I could go on with your help, that is for as long as you're here. And don't think I'm not grateful. A breathing space was essential. But at best it's muddling through on a shoestring, and if someone else can do the job better—and I believe Mr and Mrs McWilliam can —well, then I think I should get out of the way.' When Magnus did not speak she glanced at him sharply. The dumb misery she had noticed before was back in his face. 'Magnus, I *am* sorry,' she added quickly. 'I didn't think you'd mind.'

The blond head began to shake. 'It's not that. I'm sure you're right.'

Victoria drew a breath. He could only rebuff her. 'What is it, then?'

'It's me. It's what you said about getting out of the way. It's *everything*.' Magnus hurled a stone full force across the heath. '*I* want to get out of the way. I don't want Dugald to start that guide dog thing. And I know he won't listen to me. I can't think how to say it.'

It was what she had feared and Victoria's heart sank. 'Let me get this straight. You want to do something else. Is that it?'

'No,' said Magnus simply. 'I'm going blind.'

Now it was evening. Victoria had watched the lights go on in Baldougrie as she and Lorraine finished their supper. It was almost dark as she made her way up the glen. She had waited purposely, hoping that Magnus would be in bed.

'Are you quite sure Magnus said that?' Dugald repeated.

It was not the kind of statement on which you could make a mistake, but Victoria did not blame him. The first time she had heard it, she too had felt stunned.

'Yes,' she answered quietly. 'He told me he had an operation on his eyes after that accident.'

'On one eye,' Dugald corrected. 'They removed splinters of glass. They *saved* his sight. I don't know what he's thinking of.'

'But you will find out?'

'Not I. His doctor will as soon as I can get an appointment.'

That, of course, would be the best, the only way to do it. Whatever misunderstanding existed, the doctor was the right person to clear it up. Victoria felt warm again and unutterably relieved. It had been a dreadful day, quite clouding the happiness of Tango's return.

'Well, now *you* don't worry any more. Is that a promise?' Dugald took two glasses from the cupboard and a bottle with a gold and red label. She recognised the wine as the *Liebfraumilch* they had drunk with Rod and Sheila. It seemed fate was nudging her on to another subject.

'You know, you humble me.' Dugald's hand touched hers briefly as she took the glass. 'I see Magnus twenty-four hours a day and I missed what was under my nose. You never cease to surprise me, soldier. Here's to your infinite variety.'

'I think I may be going to surprise you again,' Victoria said evenly. 'Wild Heart can be yours any time, if you still want it. I've decided to sell.'

Surprise was no word, she knew he was utterly astonished. He set down the wine glass and sat himself opposite her.

'Say that again,' he invited incredulously.

There was certainly no sign of the pleasure she had expected. She watched mesmerised as he got up and poured himself a large Scotch. 'What changed you?'

'You, for one thing. The night you introduced me to Rod and Sheila. Myself for another.'

'You're going back to Fleet Street?'

'Not specifically.' London wasn't really far enough from Strathfin.

'Victoria,' he said roughly, 'if it's that game of chess you're thinking of, forget it. You've every right to Wild Heart. I'd like you to stay.'

He had had a jolt over Magnus and she thought he had a conscience over her. And soon she would be his young sister-in-law, an added reason for protecting her from herself. But, crazily, it was him Victoria wanted to protect. And look after. And love.

'Thank you,' she said gently. 'But my reasons are—personal.'

Craig called next morning to say there would be no clinic on Tuesday because he was taking a few days' holiday. Victoria swallowed her annoyance, though she felt uncomfortably certain Aunt Elizabeth would have shown more guts. In any event, the days of the clinic in its present form were numbered. Rod and Sheila had a mobile dispensary unit which would now take Strathfin into its orbit.

To her amazement Craig's face went dark when he heard this. 'How come? Why am I being cut off? I've sweated my guts out here every Tuesday for years.'

She realised a little faintly that he was quite serious. 'It's nothing to do with you. It's because they're taking me over.' Plans were still tentative and private. They involved making the society a grant from the Wild Heart monies; Dugald was sure Aunt Elizabeth's name could be perpetuated in some way. 'The die is cast, I'm selling. And honestly, Craig, I'm convinced I'm doing the right thing.'

A subtle change had come over Craig's face. His jaw had set like steel and his eyes had a strange glitter.

'You're selling to Dugald Douglas?' She nodded. 'Then let me unconvince you with all speed. I can get you twice the price if you leave it to me. I know people who have been after the place for years.'

It was a far from enjoyable discussion. Craig threw out a figure which staggered her and 'upped' it when he saw her shake her head.

'It can't be worth that,' Victoria protested dazedly.

'Ducky,' Craig was exasperated, 'you are so naïve. It's demand makes values. The feller is loaded and he wants Wild Heart. I don't suppose he'll live in it much, but that's not our business.'

Victoria had been pleased to think that Wild Heart would have a good owner and a whole-time tenant. Dugald wanted the house for his young manager who was getting married at Christmas. Money alone would never sway her, and she said so gently but firmly.

'You're a *fool*,' Craig said furiously. It was his last word.

She felt uneasily that until that moment she had never really known him.

Or known herself like this. In six years of change there was the debris of more than one love affair, but none on which she had not been able to turn the key quickly and sensibly. This love was different. She could not get away from the moment at Drummers Pool when Dugald had let fly: '*I don't want you down here, you least of all.*'

Reason told her that the situation would be worse if he had grown fond of her because it was unthinkable that Lorraine should be hurt again, but somehow nothing stood against that misery of truth.

To her shame, it marred Ellen's call to select a replacement for the cat which had had to be put down.

The Baldougrie housekeeper had time on her hands this weekend. Dugald, she reported, had dashed off to Edinburgh on Friday, taking Magnus with him and had phoned to say that they would be staying over until Monday.

'Mrs Douglas was trying to get tickets for the Tattoo,' Ellen commented. 'Magnus will like that.'

It was a piece of good news, indicating that by now Magnus's fears could well be over, and it also explained why Lorraine had not yet made the promised confidence. Unconsciously Victoria sighed.

She was embarrassed when Ellen remarked on it: 'Forgive me, I know it is not my business, but is everything all right?'

'I don't suppose it ever can be,' Victoria answered honestly. 'Except in a fairytale. I know it has all worked out very well, but it's making me very sad to leave Strathfin.'

'It's making a lot of us sad to see you go, Mr Douglas included.'

Victoria's head shook. 'That's one thing I don't have —his good opinion. He made that quite clear. Not that it's worth talking about. My part is over. I was the go-between. The real ones to benefit are the animals, so two wrongs have made a right after all. The way my aunt came by Wild Heart was wrong and so was the way Dugald tried to get her out.'

There was a startled silence. 'I do not think I can have heard you right,' Ellen said with a gasp. '*Mr Douglas*? Oh, how could you think such a thing? It was Mr Maxwell went to the Council.'

Victoria stared. 'How do you know?'

'Well, I do not *know*, I couldnae swear to it, but I am as sure as makes no difference. One night I saw him round the back with two of the men on the Council taking a good look. It was just after he had made her an offer for Wild Heart and she had refused it. Some man he knew wanted it for his holidays and would be paying him a fat commission, I don't doubt.'

'Why didn't you tell me before?'

'I was not independent when you asked me. My poor old pussy was alive then and a patient. Mr Maxwell always said to come back for another injection. I thought they were doing him good and I was afraid.'

'Yes,' Victoria said gently. 'Yes. I see.'

'And there is another thing,' Ellen went on. 'I couldnae swear to it, but see you, I am quite certain. The body that went to the solicitor and paid the fine for her was Mr Douglas.'

'And what makes you think that?' Victoria hardly recognised her scratchy voice.

She saw Ellen's hand close on the kitten she had chosen. 'Because when I saw how fashed she was, I went and asked him was there anything he could do.'

Victoria dropped Ellen at the door of her little house and drove slowly home. It needed only this to brim the cup. She had been taken in by the two-timer and had shilly-shallied over the man she loved, analysing instead of trusting the dictates of her heart. 'And Craig calls me naïve,' she thought bitterly.

When she reached Wild Heart Lorraine was at the gate and had obviously been watching for the car. She looked flushed and excited and very very happy.

'I've just had a phone call.' Her lips, Victoria noticed, were all the time breaking into a smile. This, beyond all shadow of doubt, was *it*.

Lorraine hustled her into the sittingroom and pushed her into a chair. 'Sit down. Take a breath. You'll need it. I'm getting married on Monday.'

On Monday morning a number of people saw a particular car on the A7 heading south from Selkirk to the

Border. It was a big car, white and dusty, and it was giving all it had got. As it came up in mirror after mirror, the drivers concerned pulled back and let it go.

The man in the white car was alone and driving tensely, eyes fixed on the road, hands gripping the wheel. He passed Hawick and accelerated to flash through Teviotdale and on to the moors beyond. At Langholm he crossed the Esk. There were twenty-one miles to go. He made his first defined movement, took out a handkerchief and wiped his forehead. It was open country to Canonbie. With the needle quivering at eighty, he heard the whine of a police car.

The officer was young. He said what he had to, examined licence and insurance certificate and passed them back. 'I'm afraid I shall have to report this, sir. You were doing eighty-two on that stretch.'

'I know. I'm sorry. It's an emergency.'

'Trouble, sir?'

'No, not trouble. A wedding I mustn't be late for.'

The Border is a mile from Canonbie. The white car went over it at fifteen minutes to twelve.

The wedding was at noon. Lorraine's dress, purchased in Selkirk at the last minute, was blue; she had borrowed the flower-trimmed straw hat Victoria had bought for a garden party in Melbourne—everything else was old.

And so was the love, Victoria thought emotionally, as she sat in the register office and watched her sister become Mrs Michael Barnes.

Why the truth had not occurred to her earlier, she would never know. It should have done; Lorraine was not the fickle type. As soon as she had found her feet, she had written to Michael suggesting that if he still wanted to talk he should telephone and indicating the night of Dugald's dinner party as a time when she would be alone.

'*That* day! I knew you were jumpy. I thought you'd quarrelled with Dugald,' Victoria had interposed.

'That was idiotic. I think I said so.' Lorraine had gone on with the story. Michael had phoned and they had made it up. He had come twice to Wild Heart while Victoria was in Paris.

The secrecy had been a gesture. Michael would have agreed to have the wedding in London, but she was determined to prove that he was her sole essential. 'I wasn't going to make the same mistake again. I told him to get the licence and give whatever notice they wanted and we'd do it as simply as possible. And do you know something, it's ten times better without all the fuss and palaver. Oh, Vic,' her voice had softened, 'I know you got the wrong idea before, but I still mean it—I owe you a huge debt for transplanting me and forcing me to grow.'

Victoria's mind had gone over the conversation many times; she thought of it again as Michael and Lorraine sat in front of the registrar and made their declarations. It was just six weeks since the last time she and her sister had driven into Carlisle on their way to Scotland, and in the interim each of them had changed.

Lorrie would find it hard to believe, for instance, that at this moment Victoria was feeling terribly sorry for Aunt Helen and even worrying about her. She was also regretting that today, super as it was, could not have taken place in the church at Strathfin among all their friends. They were what she missed most today. One above all. If Dugald were to walk into the room at that moment, it would make it a different place.

The odd thing was how near she suddenly felt to him.

Michael's father had gone into hospital some weeks ago and his condition was serious, but he had been delighted that the wedding was on again. The plan was that Michael should take Lorraine to see him straight

from the register office and after that rejoin Victoria and
Bill, the other witness, for a meal. Bill, an old school
friend of Michael's, was flatteringly pleased to have
Victoria in his care. He had already sprinkled her
generously with confetti and as Michael and Lorraine
drove off he took her arm to pilot her to the car.

What was happening to her that night? he asked
solicitously.

Victoria was going back to Wild Heart as soon as
Michael and Lorraine had left the hotel, but when she
said this Bill would have none of it. At least, he insisted, she must have dinner with him.

Victoria opened her mouth to explain that she would
have to relieve Ellen, the cat and dog sitter, and shut it
again, speechless.

A man had stepped off the opposite pavement and
was dodging the traffic in an attempt to cross. The grey
lounge suit made him look different, citified, with long
straight legs. He zigzagged between two cars and she
held her breath. And then he sprang on to the pavement and hurried towards them. Something dreadful
must have happened, he looked so shaken. His mother?
Magnus? But then why would he be here? And then it
flashed on her that it was *Lorraine*. He had heard
about the wedding and had come hoping to make her
change her mind.

'Oh, Dugald,' Victoria said tremulously, her heart
wrung with pity.

Something seemed to die in his face. 'I see I'm late.'

'Yes. I'm very sorry.' She could think of nothing else
to say. It was all such a shock. He was a very private
person and he had thrown it all to the winds and come
all this way for nothing.

'No matter. It was a bow at a venture. I heard by
chance.'

'Well, at least you're in time for the champagne.' If

Bill suspected anything his light tone gave nothing away. 'Let's find this hotel, Vic, and have a drink while we're waiting.'

Thank heaven for nice uncomplicated people like Bill. It was embarrassing and quite ridiculous to realise that in the general rush she had let his name slip from her mind.

'Dugald, this is Bill, Mike's friend. I know what you'll think, it's just like me, I've forgotten the rest of his name.'

Bill said promptly: 'Kirkland.'

Dugald swallowed. His mouth opened and closed. He looked from the flower in Bill's buttonhole to the confetti on Victoria's hair.

'Are you telling me it's not *your* wedding today?'

A wild impossible surmise took Victoria's breath away. Again it was Bill who stepped into the breach. 'My loss, but I'm working on it. Meantime, would you excuse me for a minute. I must get some fags.'

Dugald spoke first. 'Victoria, I've got to know. You turned me down for Craig Maxwell the night of the Fashion Show and you let him make a pass at you at Drummers' Pool. Are you serious about him?'

'Serious? About *Craig*?' She blinked. 'Oh, don't be so ridiculous. Just because he saw how upset I was after you'd been so rotten . . .'

'Rotten? Me *rotten*? To *you*?'

'You said I was the last person you wanted to have around.'

'Yes, Victoria—at *Drummers' Pool*. They were a tough bunch, you could have got hurt. Anyone could, but you most of all. I was being selective, shouldn't I be? I love you.' His voice sounding quite angry died away. It came back next second. 'So if you should be thinking of a wedding day of your own, will you give me the first refusal?'

Lorraine and Michael thoroughly enjoyed their day. Dugald's presence enhanced it. He gave an edited explanation. Magnus had stayed in Edinburgh with his grandmother to see the Tattoo. Thank heaven, it *would* be a case of 'seeing'. His sight irregularity was correctible and completely unrelated to the accident, but the boy had put two and two together and made, as his uncle put it, twenty-two. 'Though it was understandable,' he added. 'We hadn't told him enough. The doctors in the hospital were concerned about his general health and recommended he should stay away from his books for an indefinite period. That's why he's been with me, not, as he seems to have concluded, to be a guinea-pig for my guide dogs. He's fine, as a matter of fact, and he'll be going back to school at the end of the month. But if it hadn't been for Victoria he could have gone on worrying for much longer.'

Magnus disposed of, he went on to say that on arriving home himself, he had inquired for Ellen and been told where she was and the reason. The temptation to gatecrash, he assured them blandly, had proved irresistible.

In the early evening the white car went north leaving Victoria's to be picked up next day by one of Dugald's staff. It was time for the true slant on the story.

Ellen, not expecting her employer before evening, had sent a friend to the castle to deputise. The friend had told Dugald that Miss Elliott was being married that morning in Carlisle and it had simply not occurred to him that it could have been Lorraine. Again an ironic coincidence. Yesterday, one of the dogs had needed attention, and Craig's locum had come. Craig away, but no one knowing where, Victoria relinquishing Wild Heart 'for personal reasons' and now gone to Carlisle to be married.

'Stop saying that. I wasn't,' Victoria protested.

'Do you blame me?'

'Yes. It's hysterical. I have no illusions about Craig. All he wants is money. I'm not even sure he didn't lose Tango on purpose so that I'd give up Wild Heart and let him have *carte blanche* to sell it. I once spoke rather foolishly about Tango and he may have stored it up. But I don't know. Let's not talk about it.' Victoria felt strongly that recriminations should be set aside and that Aunt Elizabeth, wherever she was battling at this moment, would agree with her.

In the open country near Langholm Dugald stopped the car. For some miles Victoria had known that they were in Scotland. Lochinvar's 'wide border' lay under a golden sky.

'There's the Esk,' she said dreamily.

'Yes. I didn't swim it. Just got booked for speeding.'

'And all for nothing. Oh dear!' Much worse could have happened in that mad dash, the thought was both horror and miraculous joy.

'For a great deal—I hope. Can you answer my question yet?'

'I think so—if you'll ask it.'

Dugald took both her hands in a gentle old-fashioned way. 'My dear, I love you and need you. Will you think about that wedding and give me the first refusal?'

'That's one thing I couldn't do, refuse you,' Victoria answered.

She had trained herself not to cry for pain or grief. Joy was different. Joy was a man's face which had suddenly gone quiet and the light in eyes that were able to read her own. It was the arms that held her, the lips that kissed her and, at the end of the road, the gates of Baldougrie wide open to welcome her home.

*Harlequin Presents...*

**By popular demand...**
36 original novels from this series—by 3 of the world's greatest romance authors.
These back issues by Anne Hampson, Anne Mather and Violet Winspear have been out of print for some time. So don't miss out; order your copies now!

*All the above titles are available at 95¢ each. Please use the attached order form to indicate your requirements.* Offer expires December 31, 1977